11/20

Copyright © 2019 by Gavin Aung Than
Original interior design by Gavin Aung Than and
Benjamin Fairclough © Penguin Random House Australia Pty Ltd.

All rights reserved. Published in the United States by Random House Children's Books, a division of Penguin Random House LLC, New York. Originally published by Puffin Books, an imprint of Penguin Random House Australia Pty Ltd., Sydney, in 2019.

Random House and the colophon are registered trademarks of Penguin Random House LLC.

Visit us on the Web! rhcbooks.com

Educators and librarians, for a variety of teaching tools, visit us at RHTeachersLibrarians.com

Library of Congress Cataloging-in-Publication Data is available upon request.
ISBN 978-0-593-17508-8 (trade pbk.)
ISBN 978-0-593-17505-7 (hardcover)
ISBN 978-0-593-17506-4 (lib. bdg.)
ISBN 978-0-593-17507-1 (ebook)

The artist used Adobe Photoshop to create the illustrations for this book.
The text of this book is set in 11-point Sugary Pancake.
This edition's cover and interior design by Sylvia Bi and colorization by Sarah Stern

MANUFACTURED IN CHINA
10 9 8 7 6 5 4 3 2 1
First American Edition

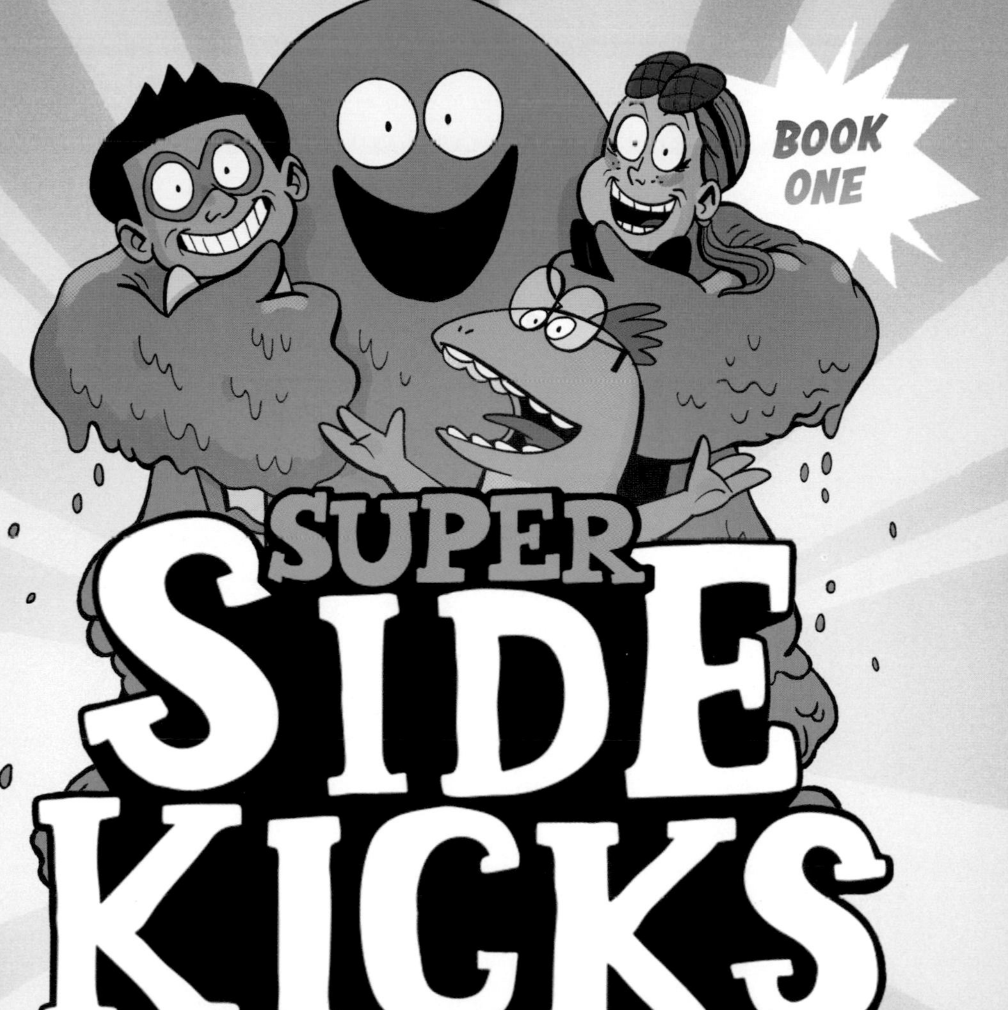

BOOK ONE

SUPER SIDEKICKS

NO ADULTS ALLOWED

Gavin Aung Than

Color by Sarah Stern

Random House New York

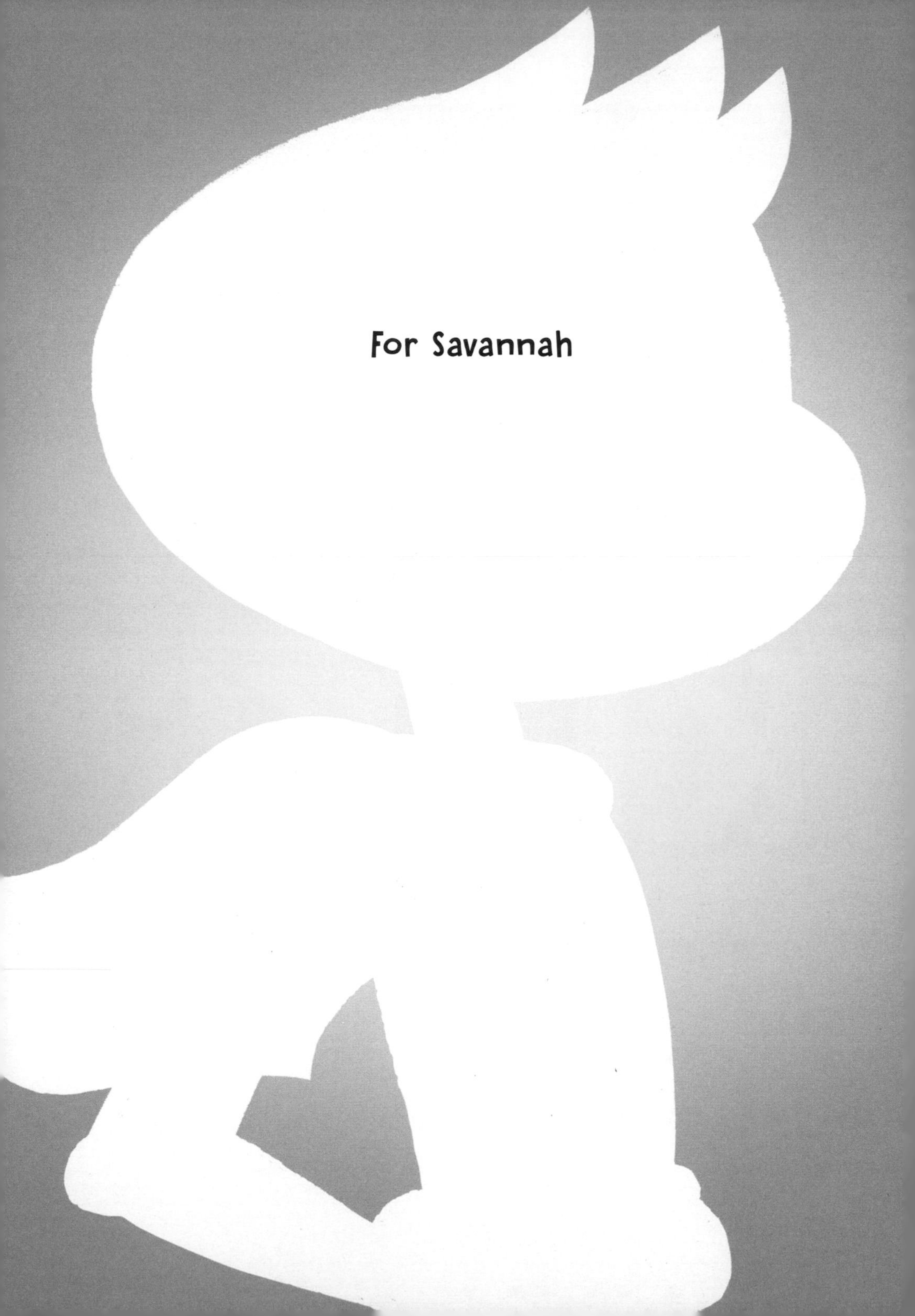

For Savannah

Chapter

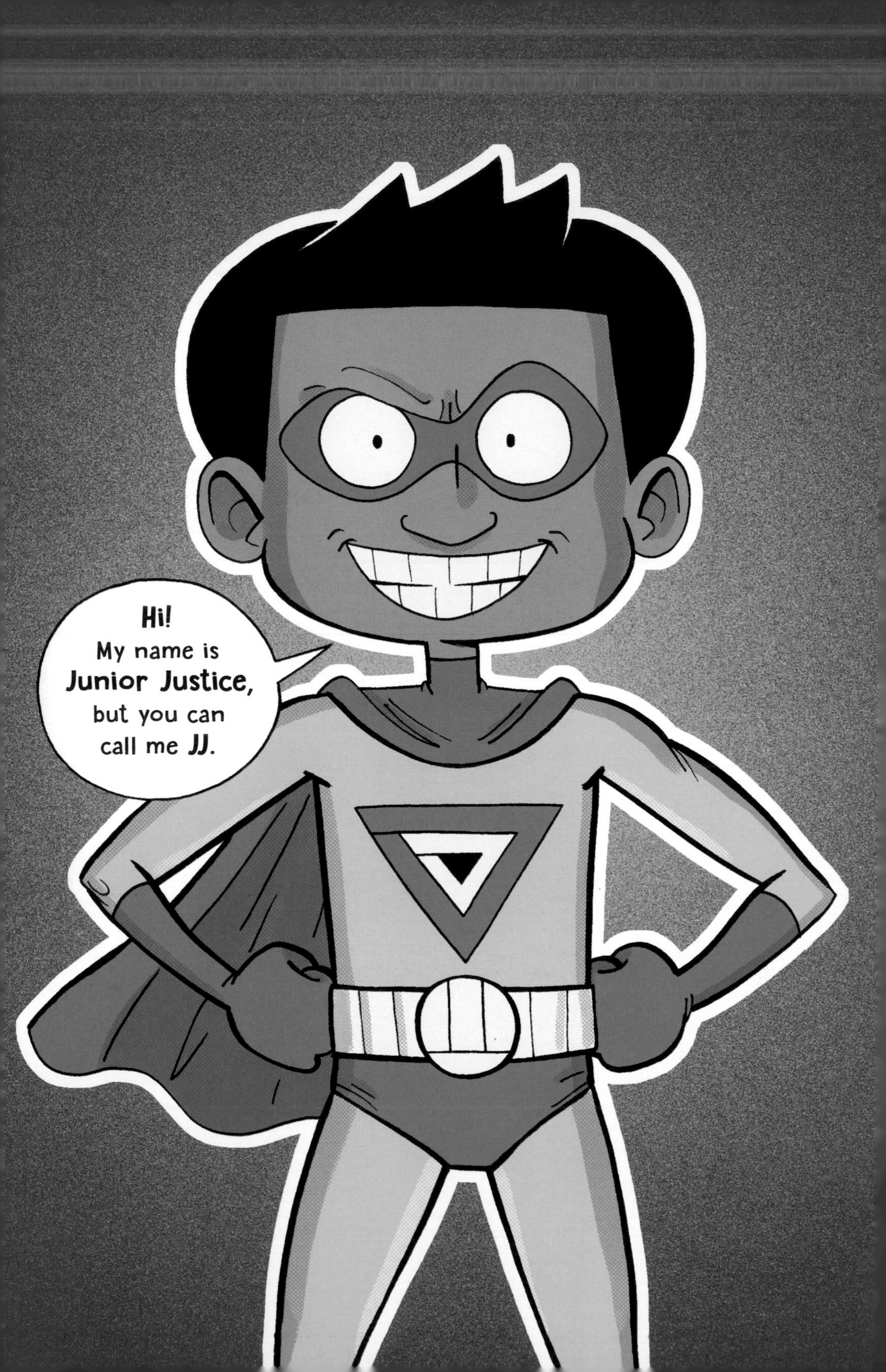
Hi!
My name is Junior Justice, but you can call me JJ.

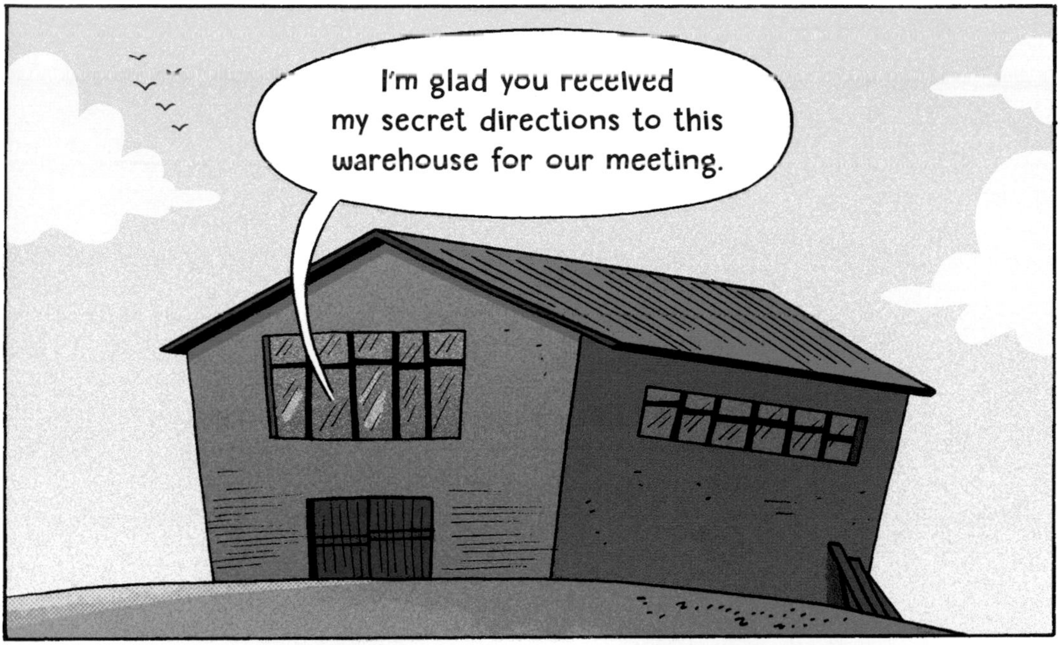
I'm glad you received my secret directions to this warehouse for our meeting.

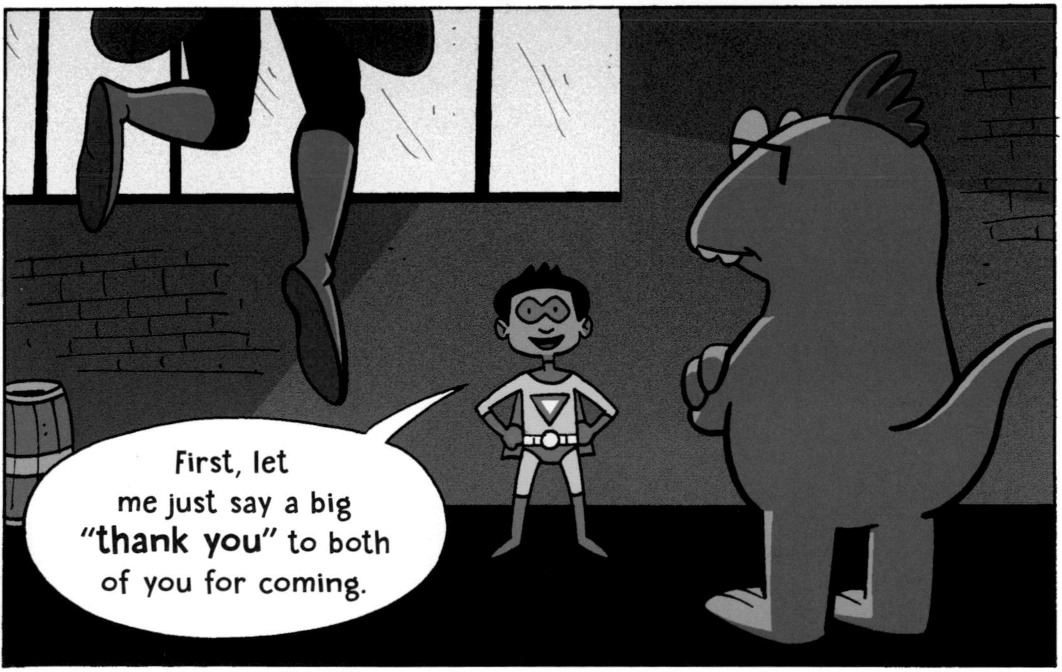
First, let me just say a big "**thank you**" to both of you for coming.

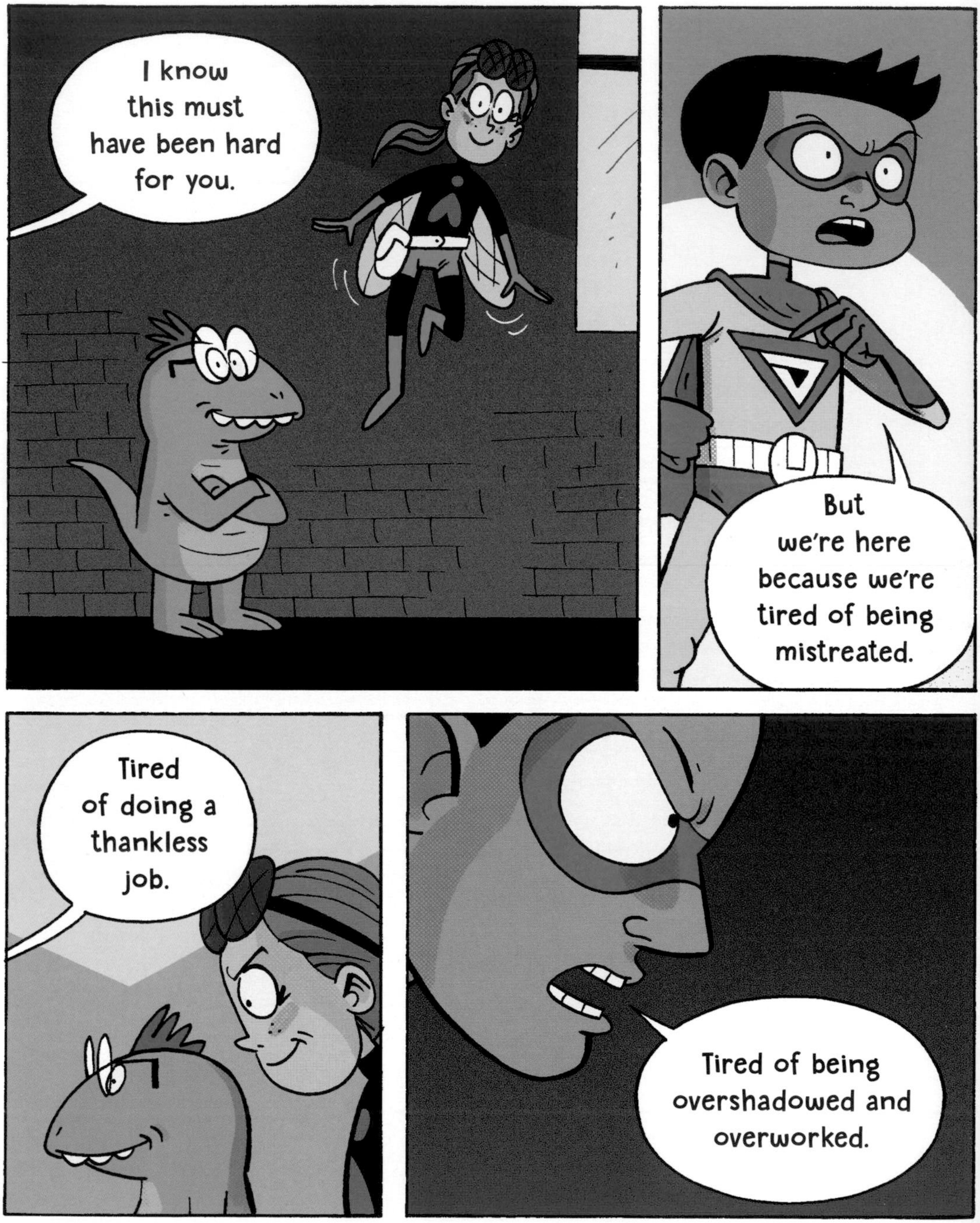
I know this must have been hard for you.
But we're here because we're tired of being mistreated.
Tired of doing a thankless job.
Tired of being overshadowed and overworked.

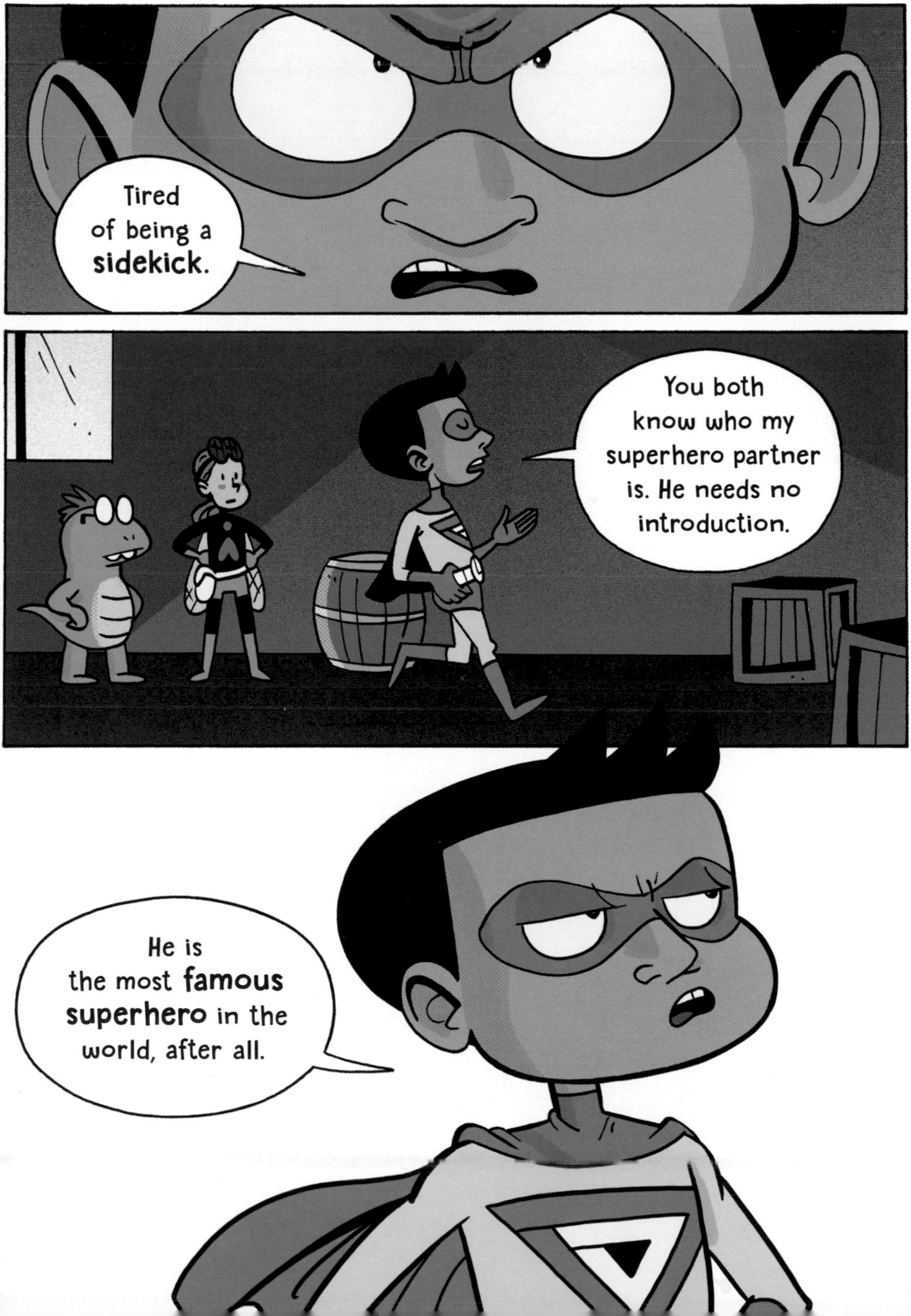
Tired of being a **sidekick**.
You both know who my superhero partner is. He needs no introduction.
He is the most **famous** **superhero** in the world, after all.

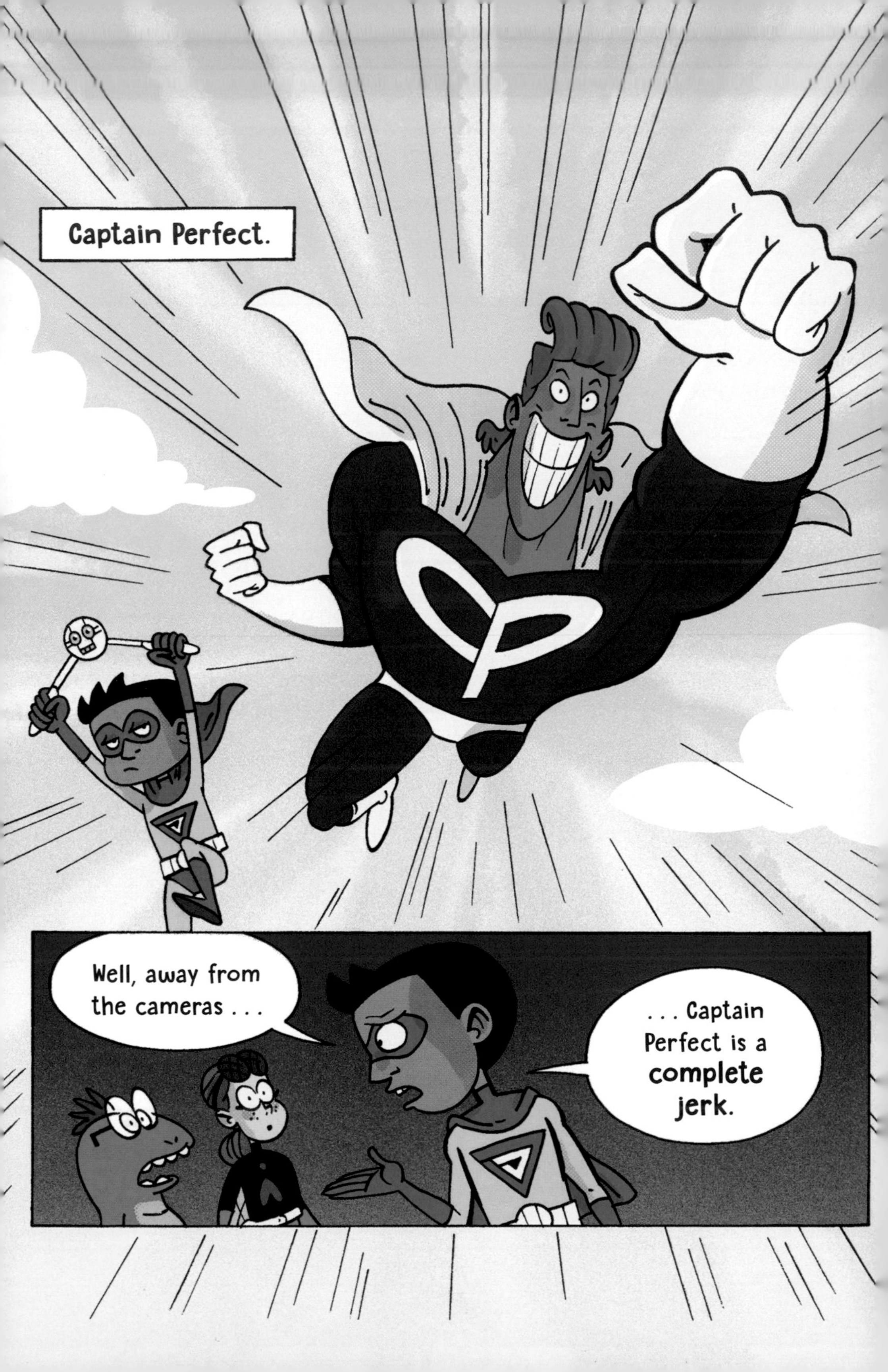
Captain Perfect.
Well, away from the cameras . . .
. . . Captain Perfect is a complete jerk.

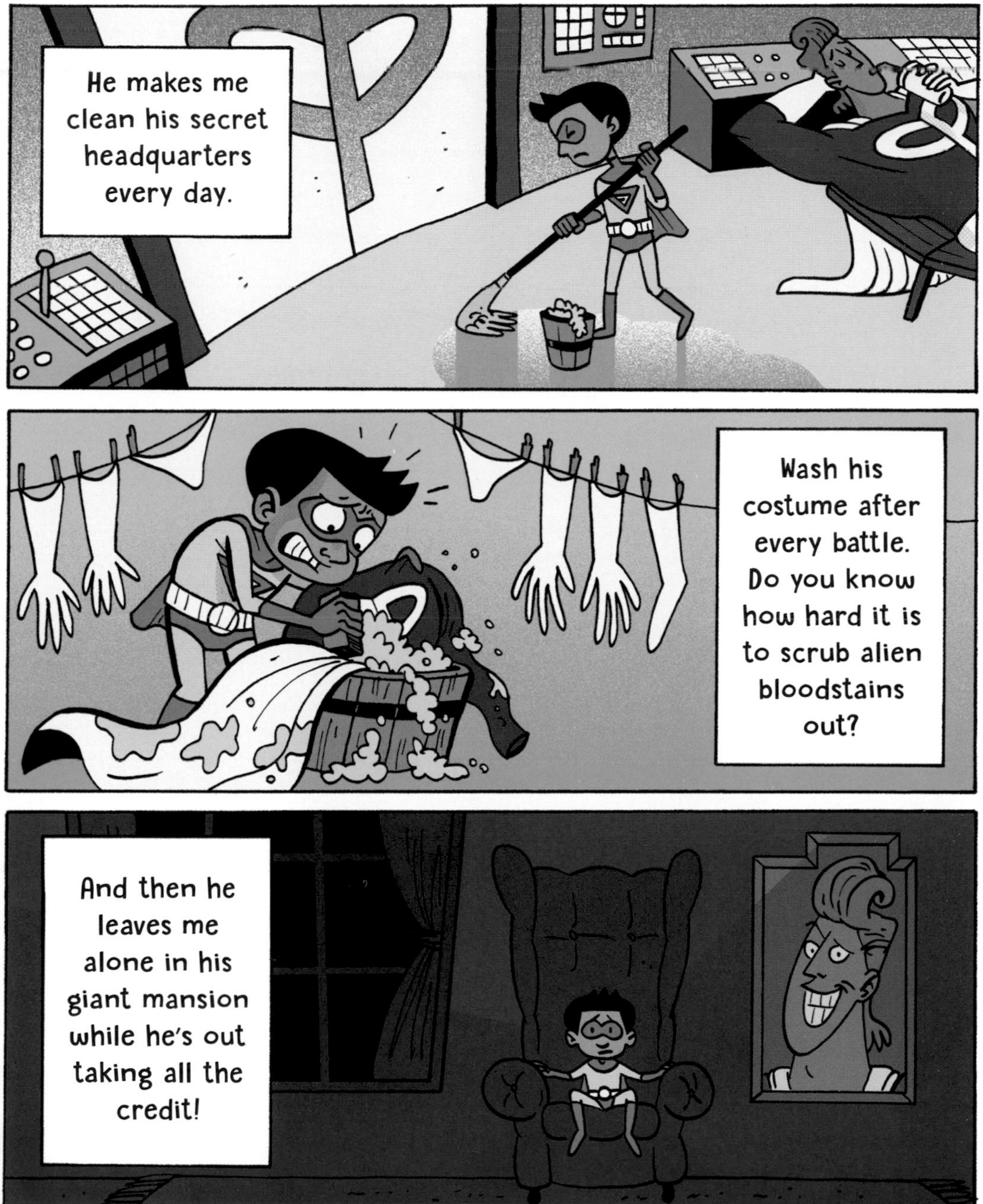
He makes me clean his secret headquarters every day.
Wash his costume after every battle. Do you know how hard it is to scrub alien bloodstains out?
And then he leaves me alone in his giant mansion while he's out taking all the credit!

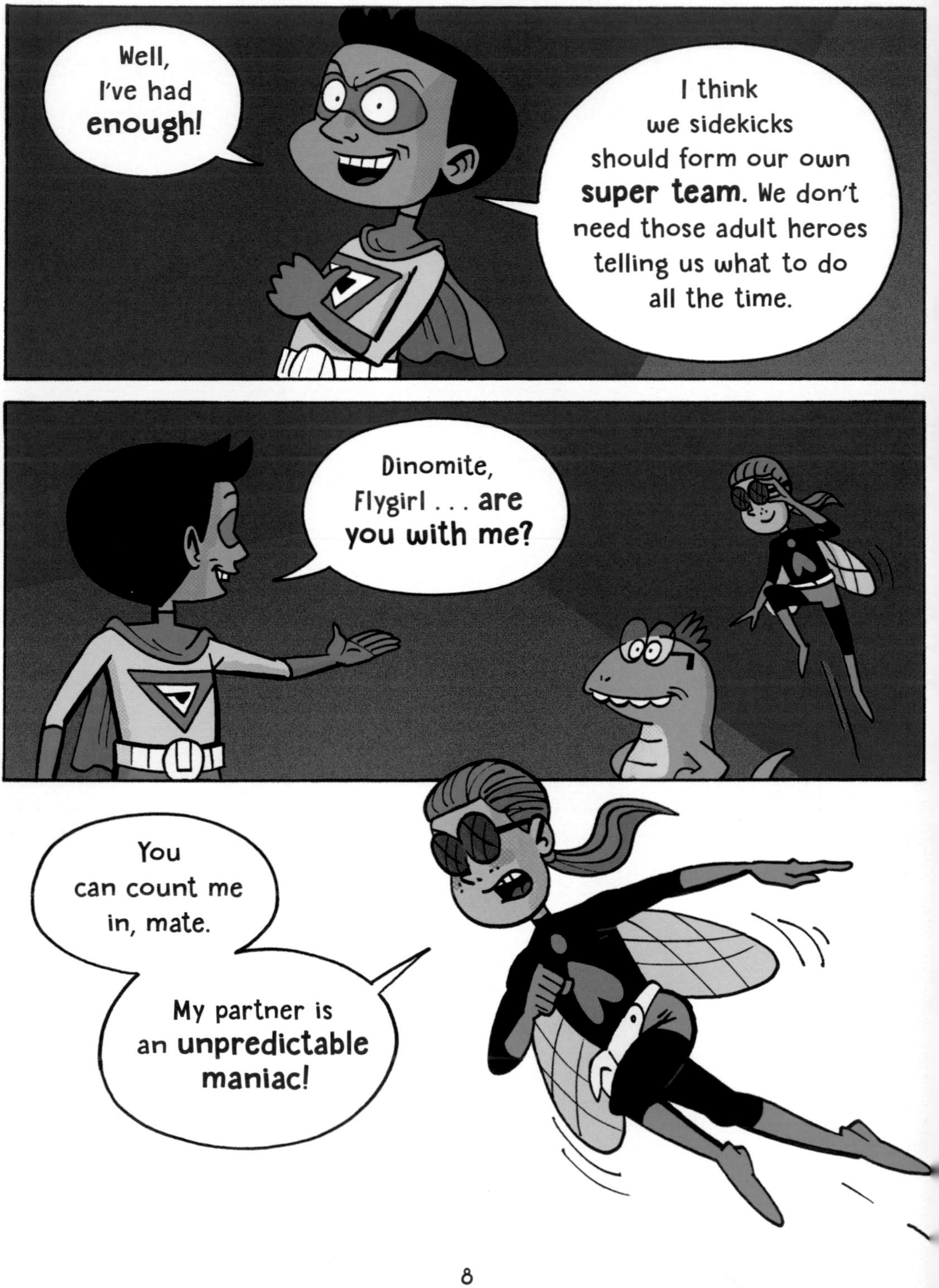
Well, I've had enough!
I think we sidekicks should form our own super team. We don't need those adult heroes telling us what to do all the time.
Dinomite, Flygirl . . . are you with me?
You can count me in, mate.
My partner is an unpredictable maniac!

I've been Rampagin' Rita's sidekick ever since I started in the business.
RITA BASH!
BOOM
She means well, but all she wants to do is bash and clobber things.

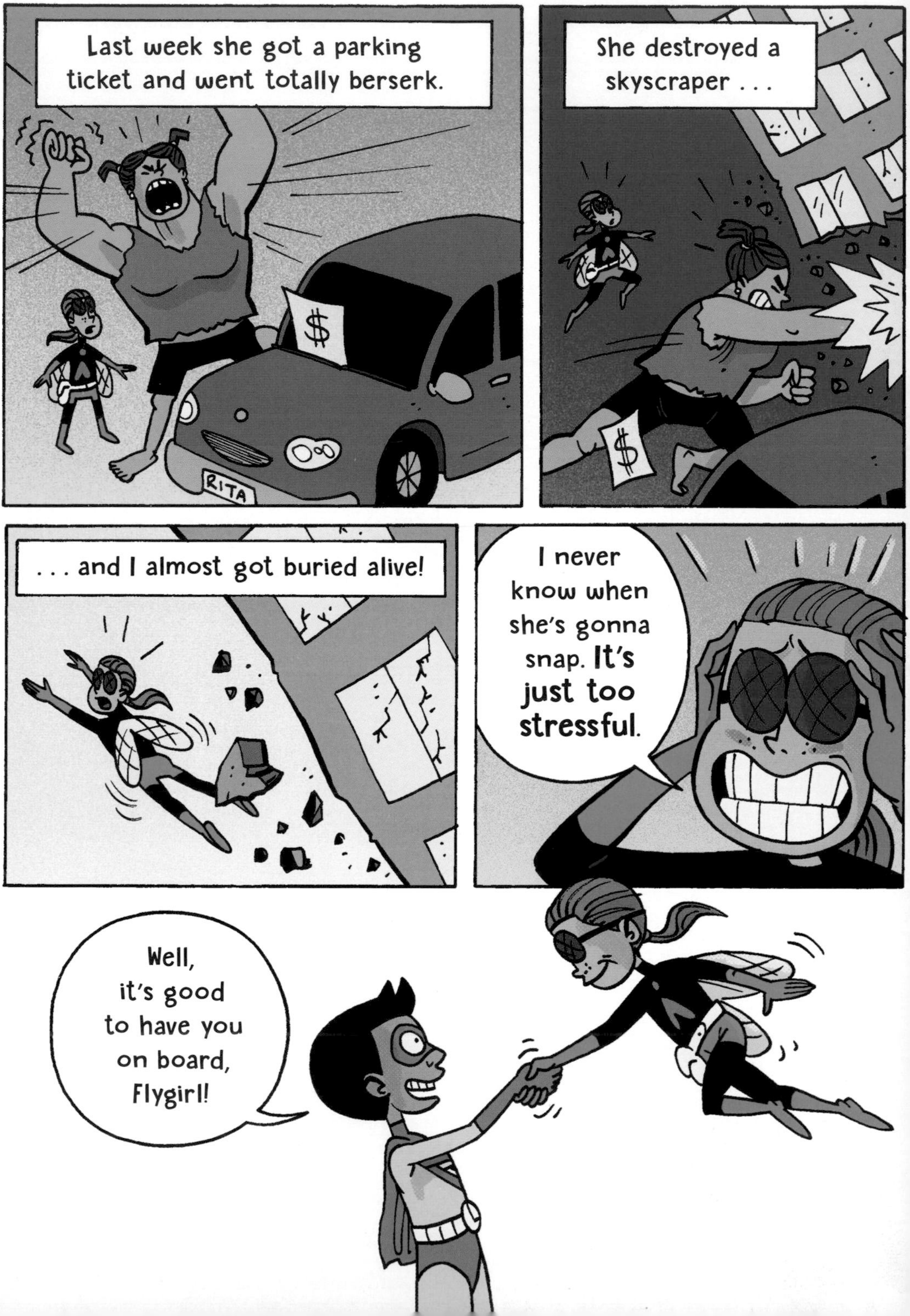
Last week she got a parking ticket and went totally berserk.
$
RITA
She destroyed a skyscraper . . .
$
. . . and I almost got buried alive!
I never know when she's gonna snap. It's just too stressful.
Well, it's good to have you on board, Flygirl!

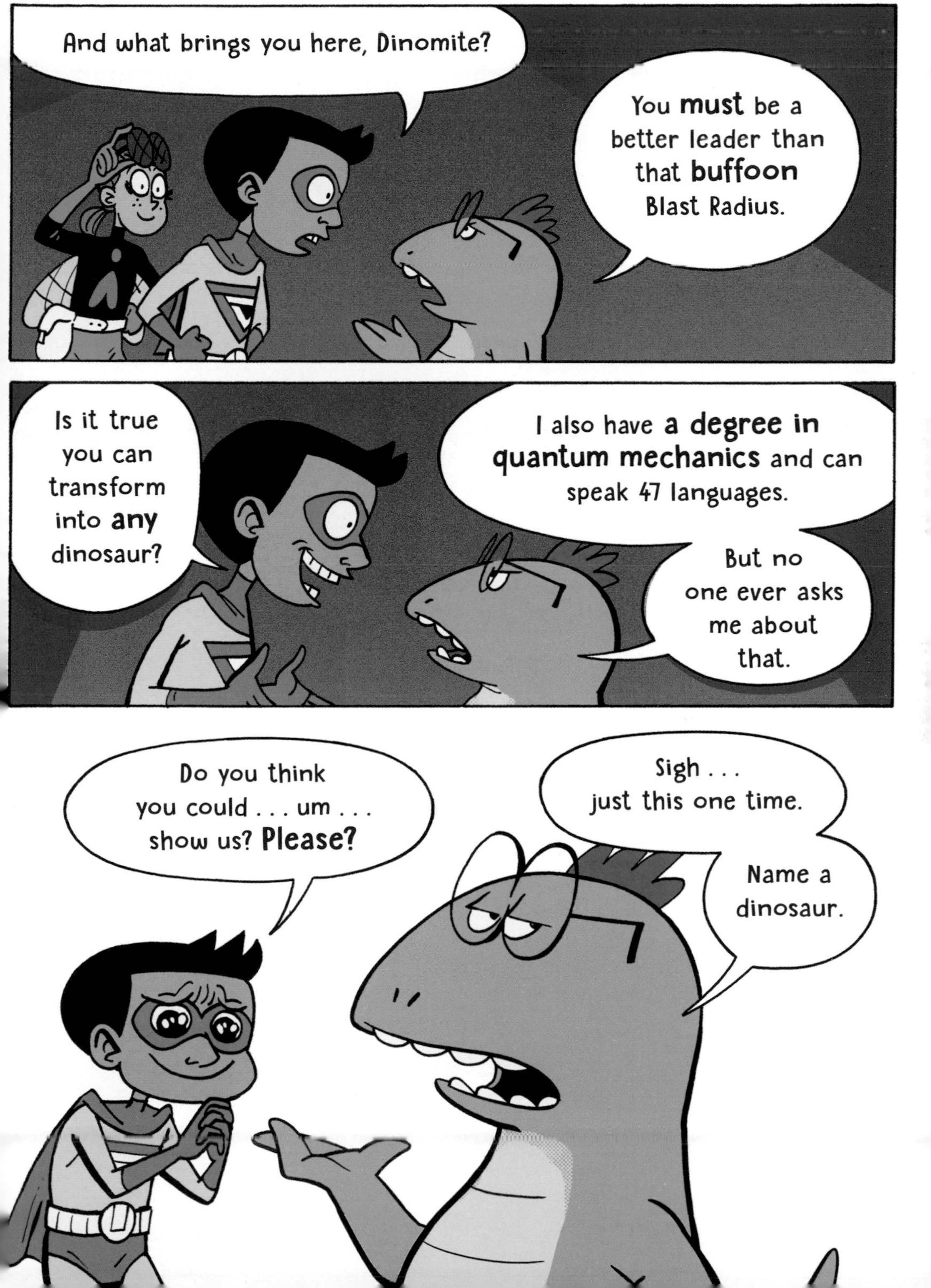
And what brings you here, Dinomite?
You **must** be a better leader than that **buffoon** Blast Radius.
Is it true you can transform into **any** dinosaur?
I also have **a degree in quantum mechanics** and can speak 47 languages.
But no one ever asks me about that.
Do you think you could . . . um . . . show us? **Please?**
Sigh . . . just this one time.
Name a dinosaur.

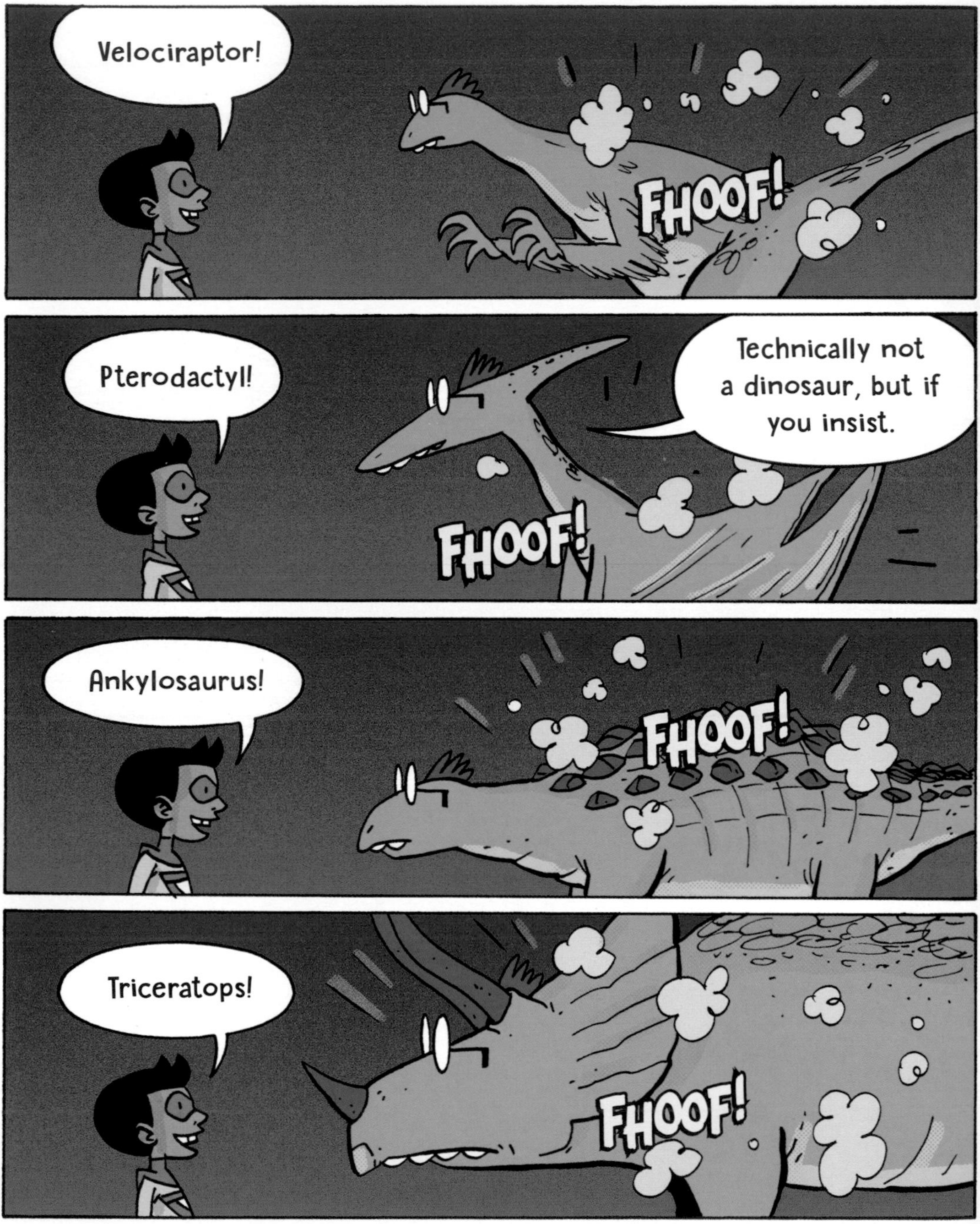

Velociraptor!
FHOOF!
Pterodactyl!
Technically not a dinosaur, but if you insist.
FHOOF!
Ankylosaurus!
FHOOF!
Triceratops!
FHOOF!

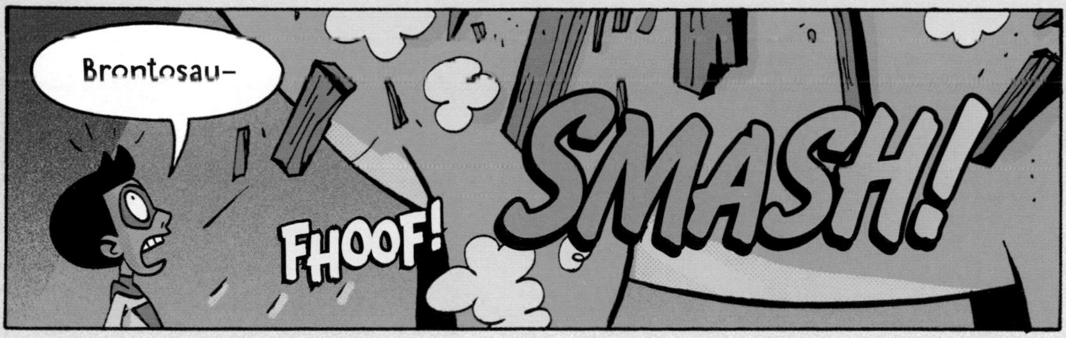
Brontosau-
FHOOF!
SMASH!

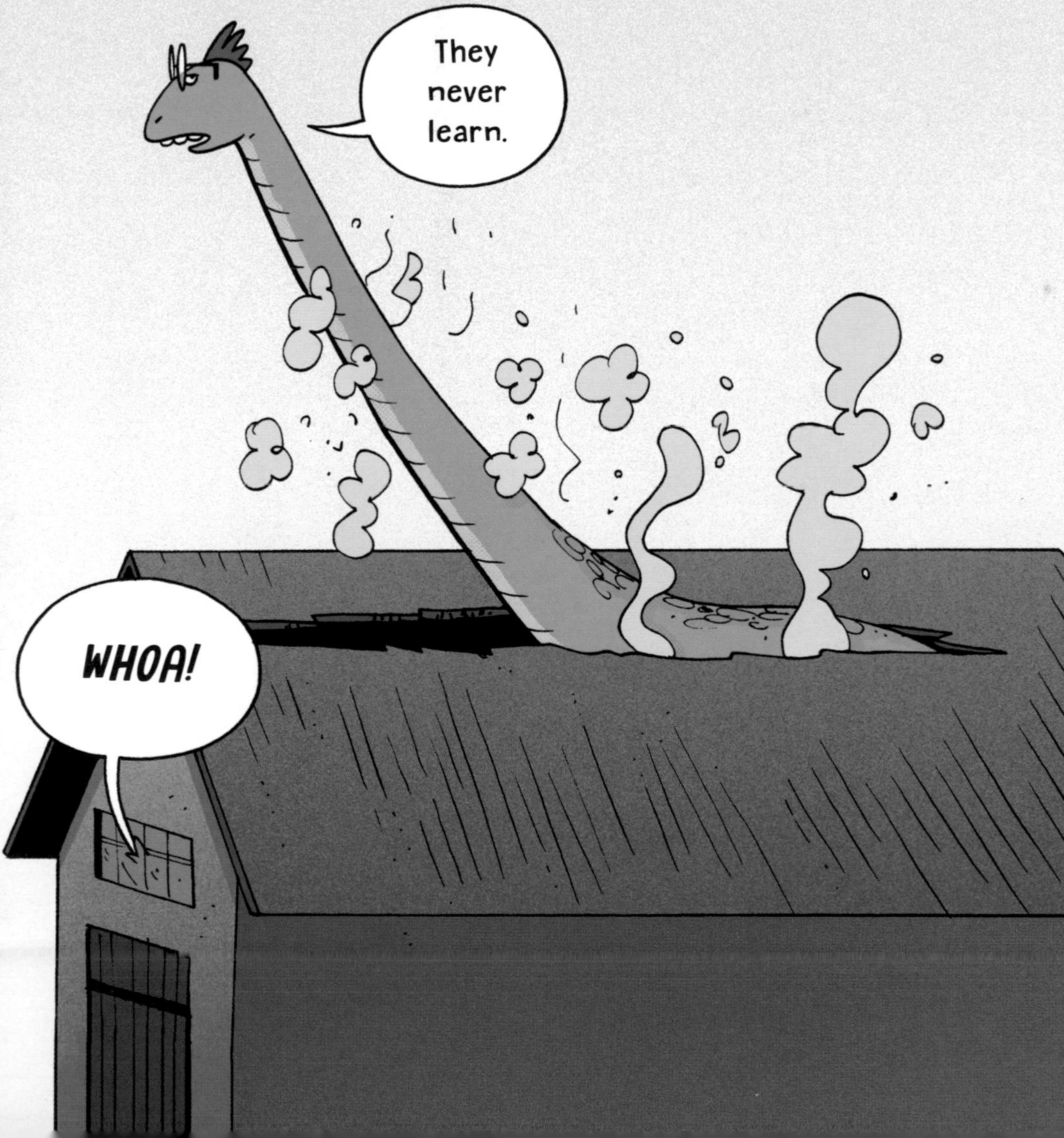
They never learn.
WHOA!

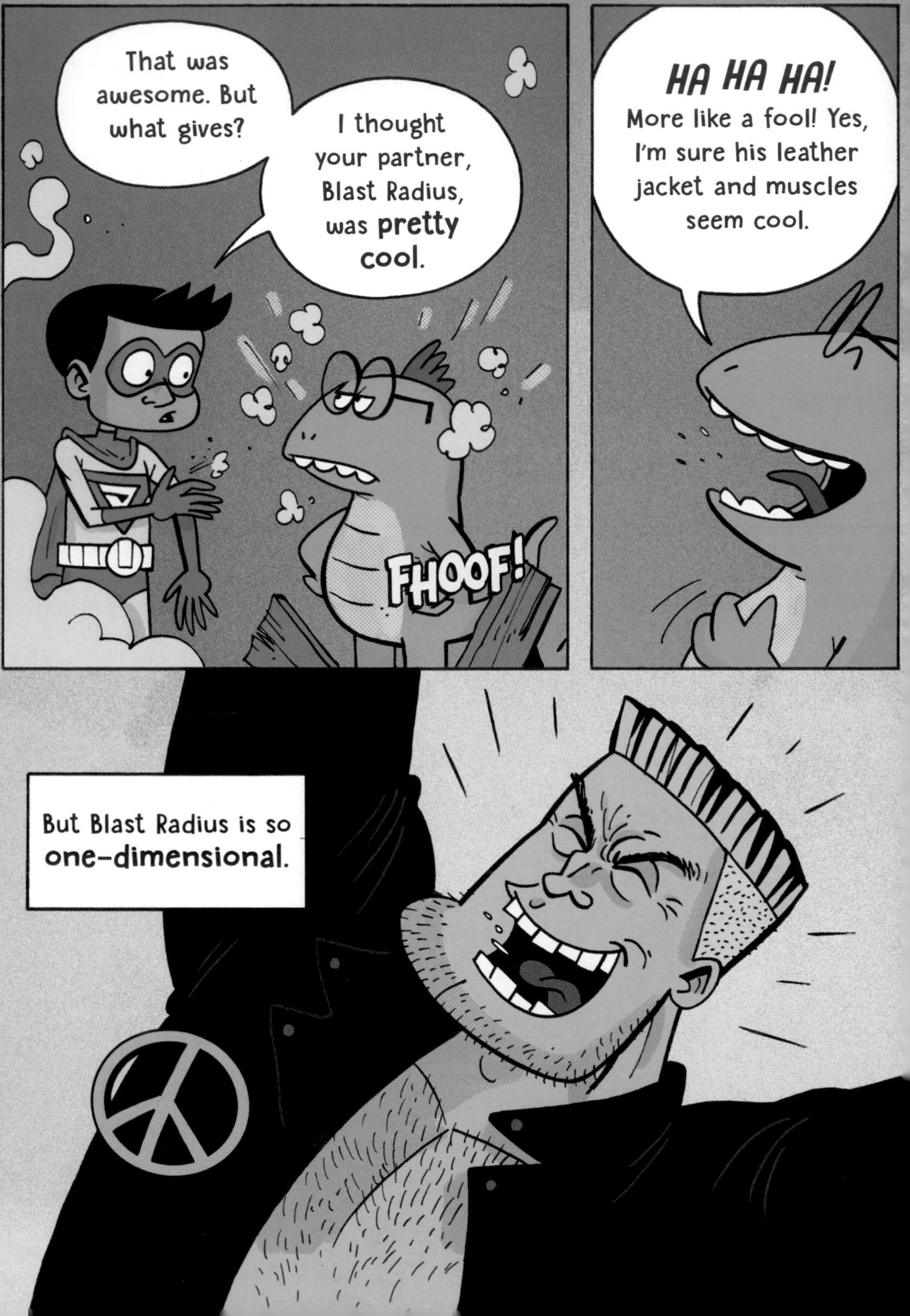

That was awesome. But what gives?
I thought your partner, Blast Radius, was pretty cool.
FHOOF!
HA HA HA!
More like a fool! Yes, I'm sure his leather jacket and muscles seem cool.
But Blast Radius is so one-dimensional.

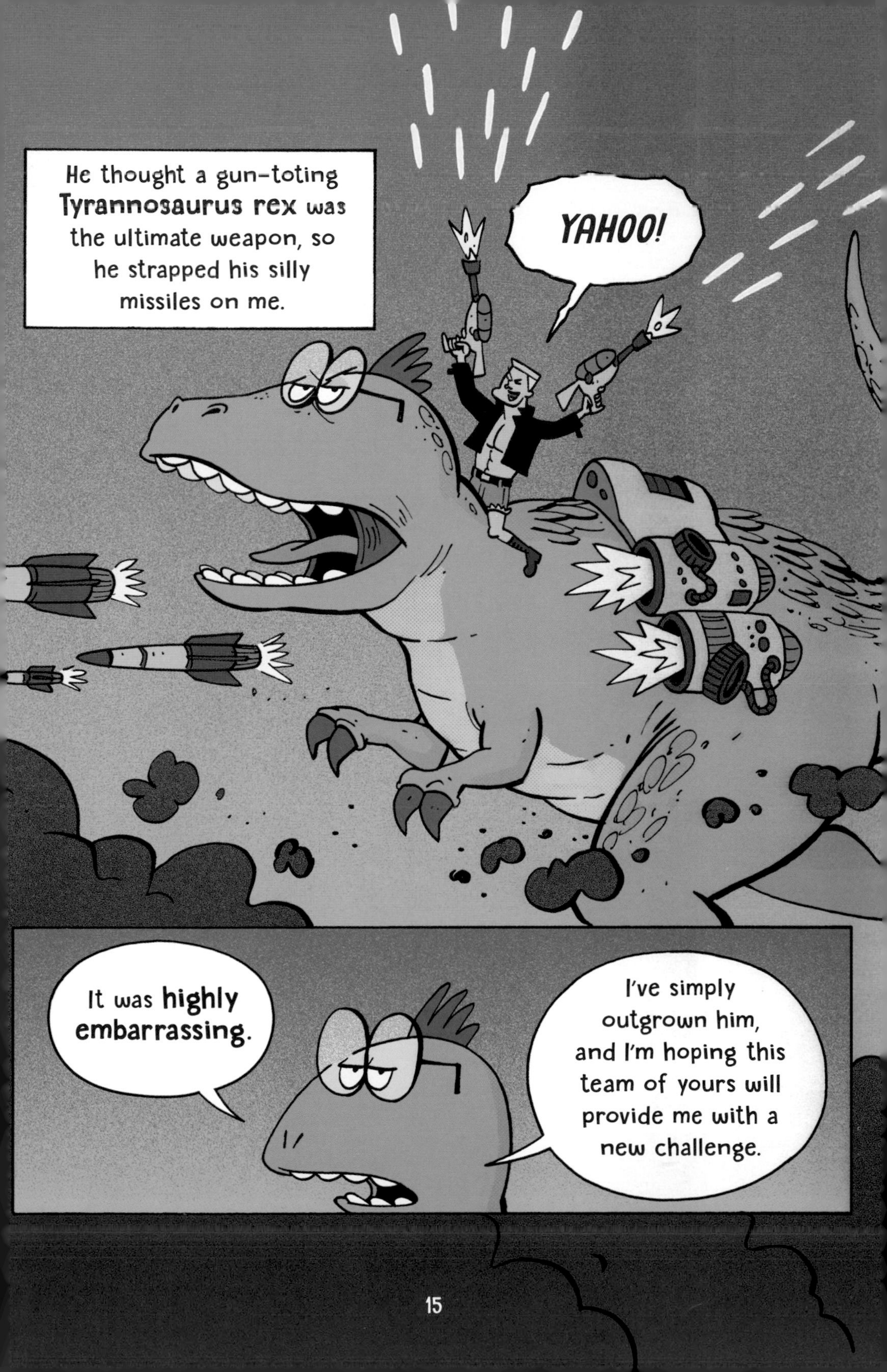
He thought a gun-toting Tyrannosaurus rex was the ultimate weapon, so he strapped his silly missiles on me.
YAHOO!
It was highly embarrassing.
I've simply outgrown him, and I'm hoping this team of yours will provide me with a new challenge.

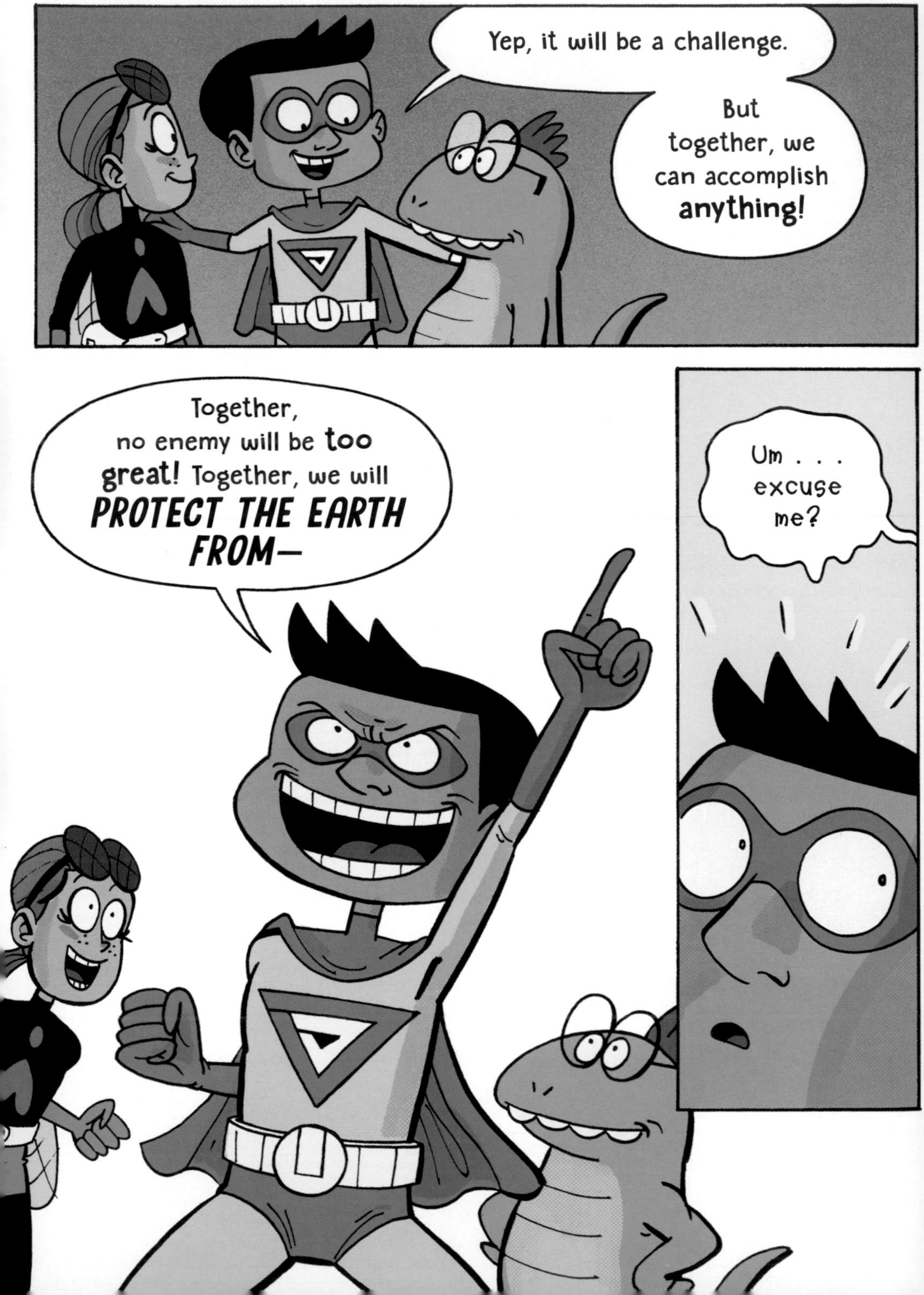
Yep, it will be a challenge.
But together, we can accomplish anything!
Together, no enemy will be too great! Together, we will PROTECT THE EARTH FROM—
Um . . . excuse me?

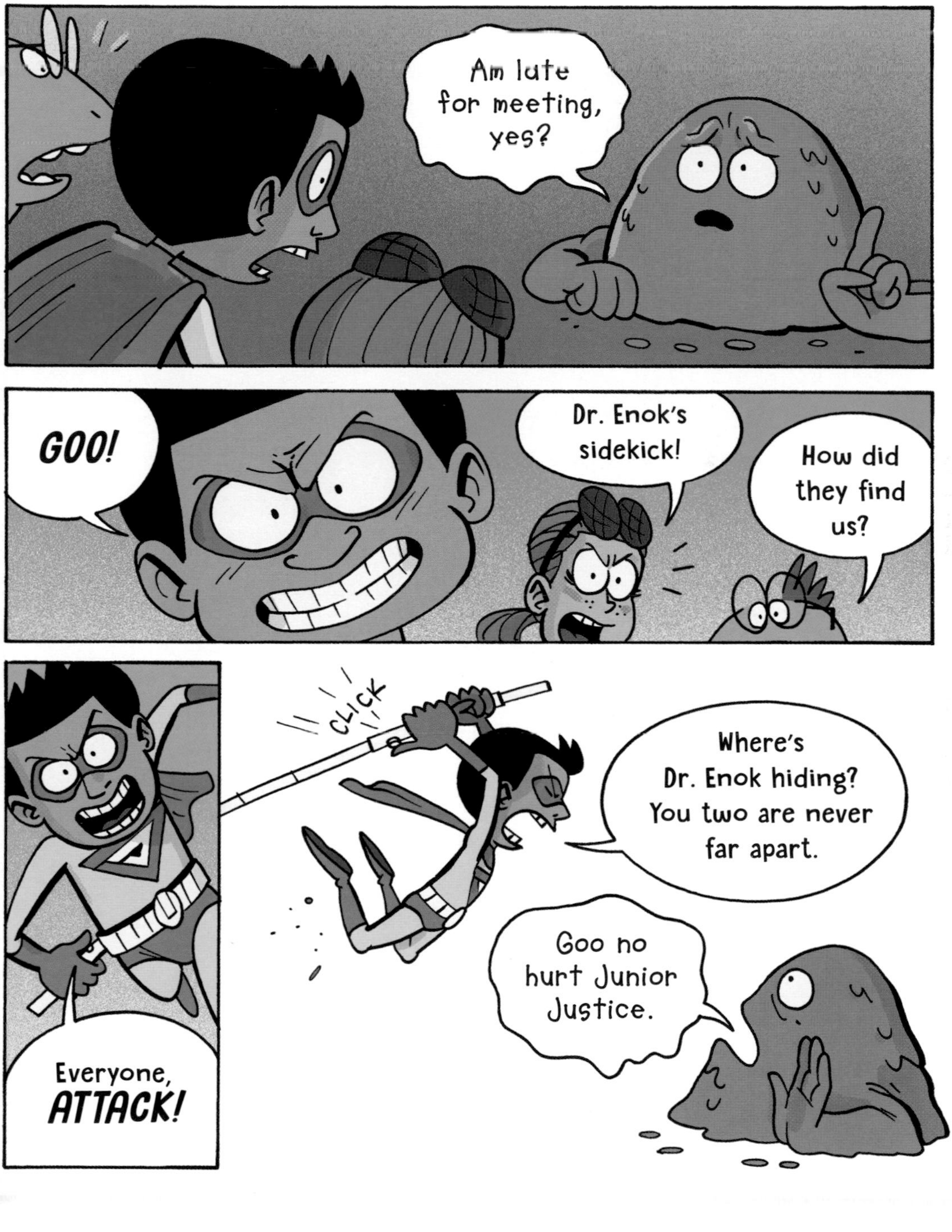
Am late for meeting, yes?
GOO!
Dr. Enok's sidekick!
How did they find us?
CLICK
Where's Dr. Enok hiding? You two are never far apart.
Goo no hurt Junior Justice.
Everyone, ATTACK!

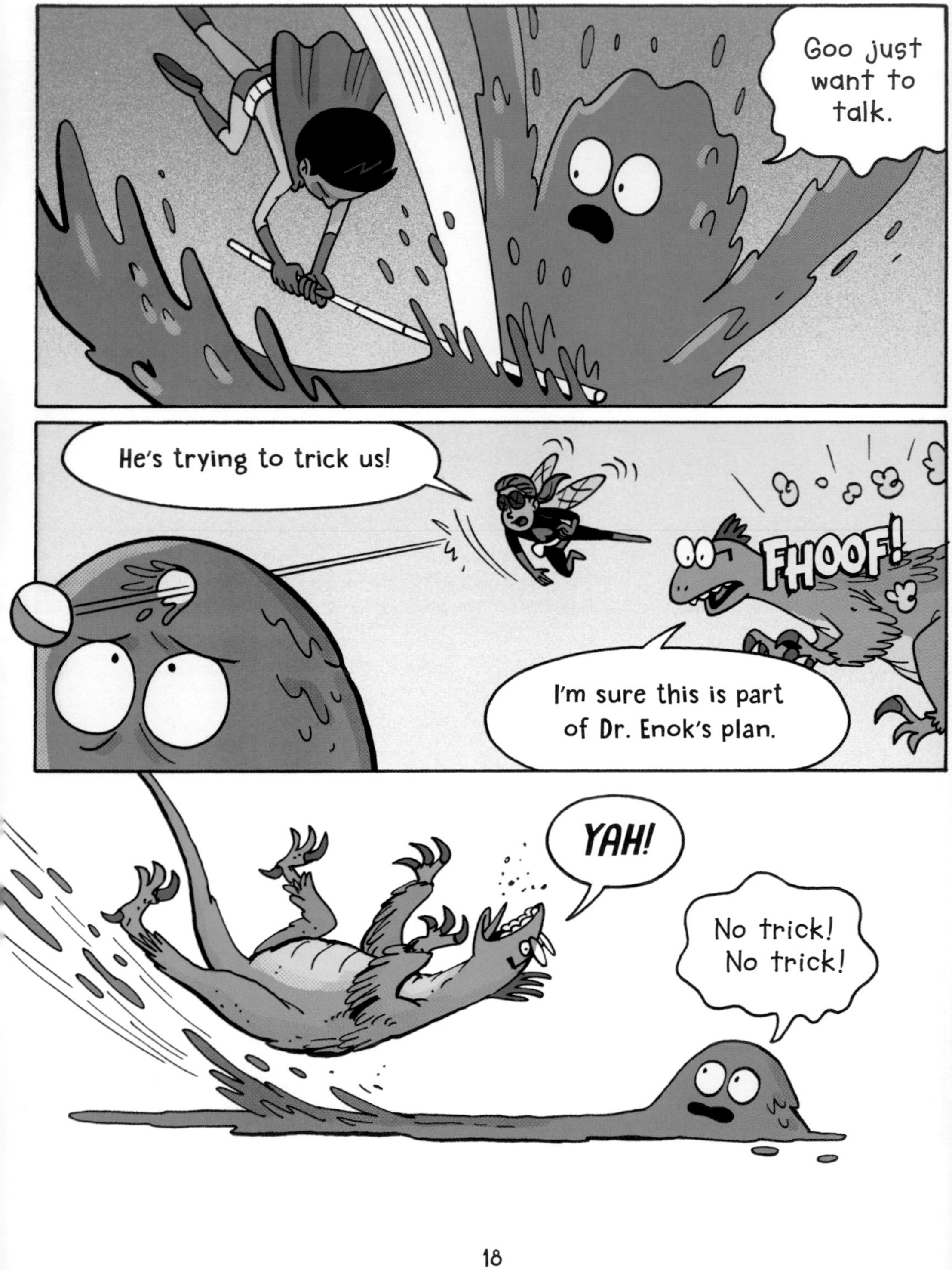
Goo just want to talk.
He's trying to trick us!
FHOOF!
I'm sure this is part of Dr. Enok's plan.
YAH!
No trick! No trick!

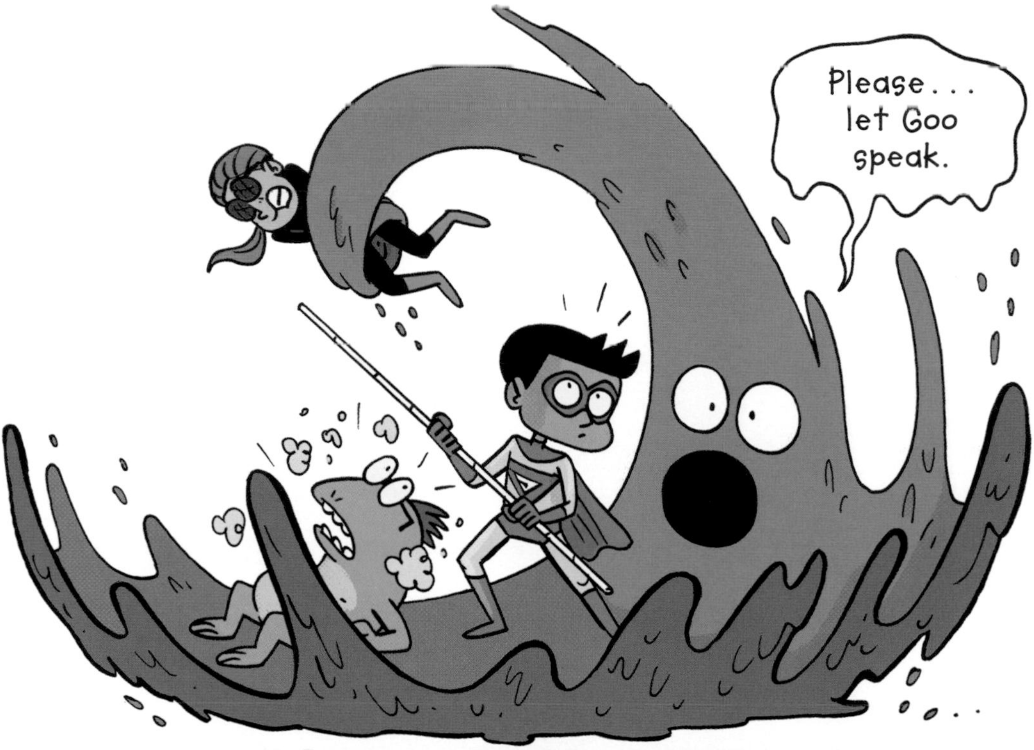
Please... let Goo speak.

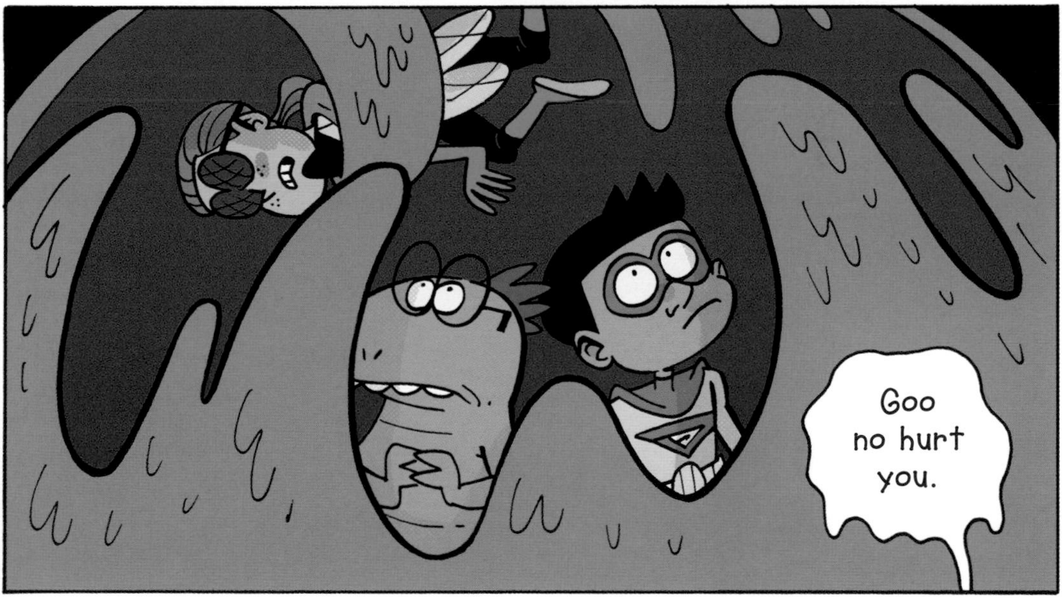
Goo no hurt you.

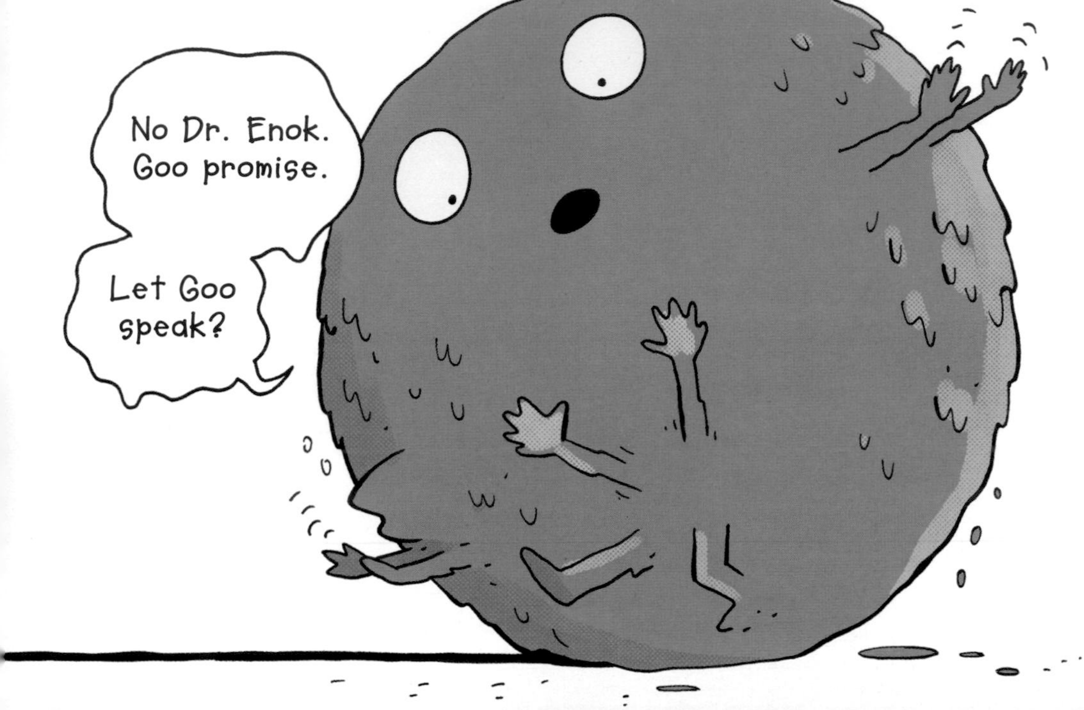
No Dr. Enok. Goo promise.
Let Goo speak?

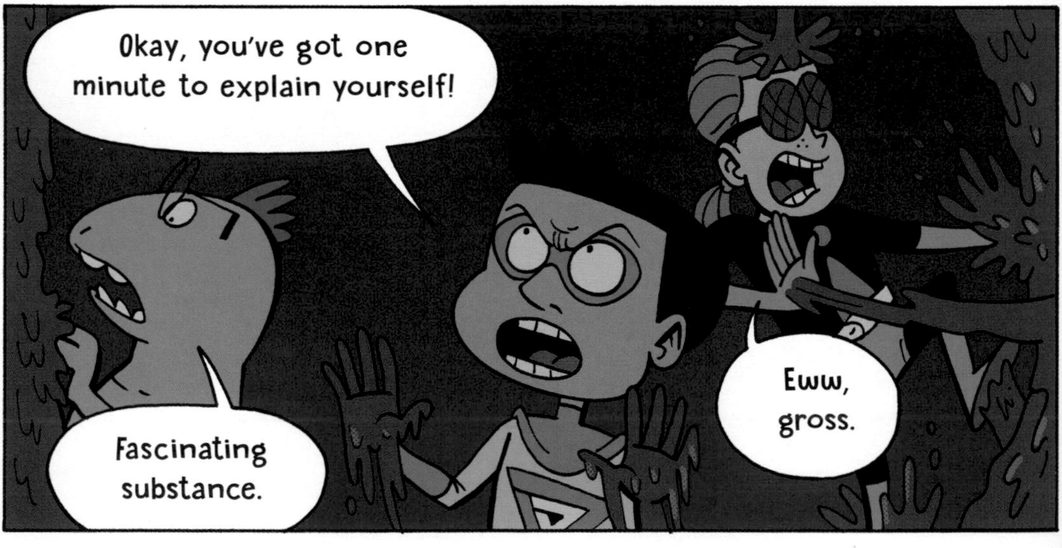
Okay, you've got one minute to explain yourself!
Fascinating substance.
Eww, gross.

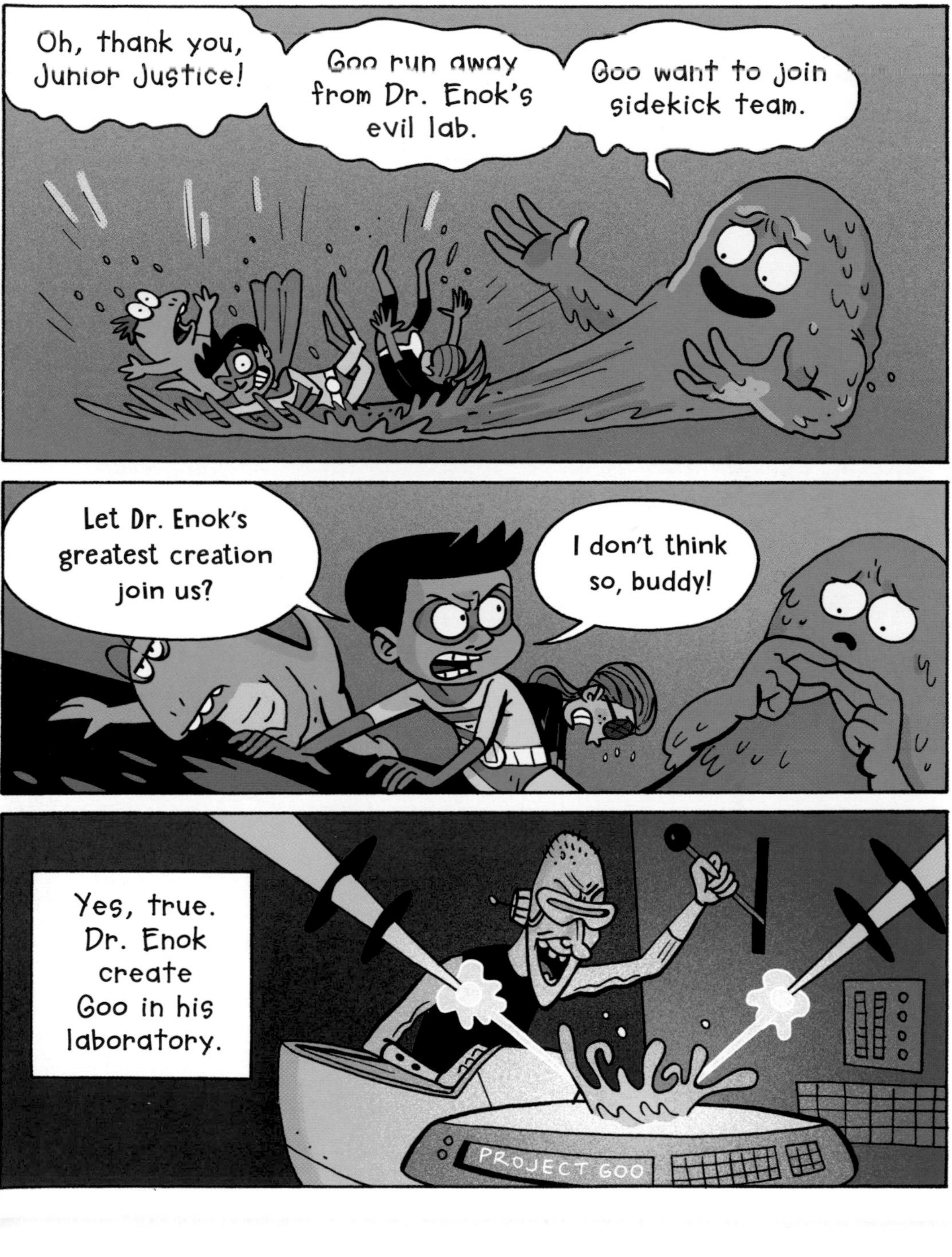
Oh, thank you, Junior Justice!
Goo run away from Dr. Enok's evil lab.
Goo want to join sidekick team.
Let Dr. Enok's greatest creation join us?
I don't think so, buddy!
Yes, true. Dr. Enok create Goo in his laboratory.
PROJECT GOO

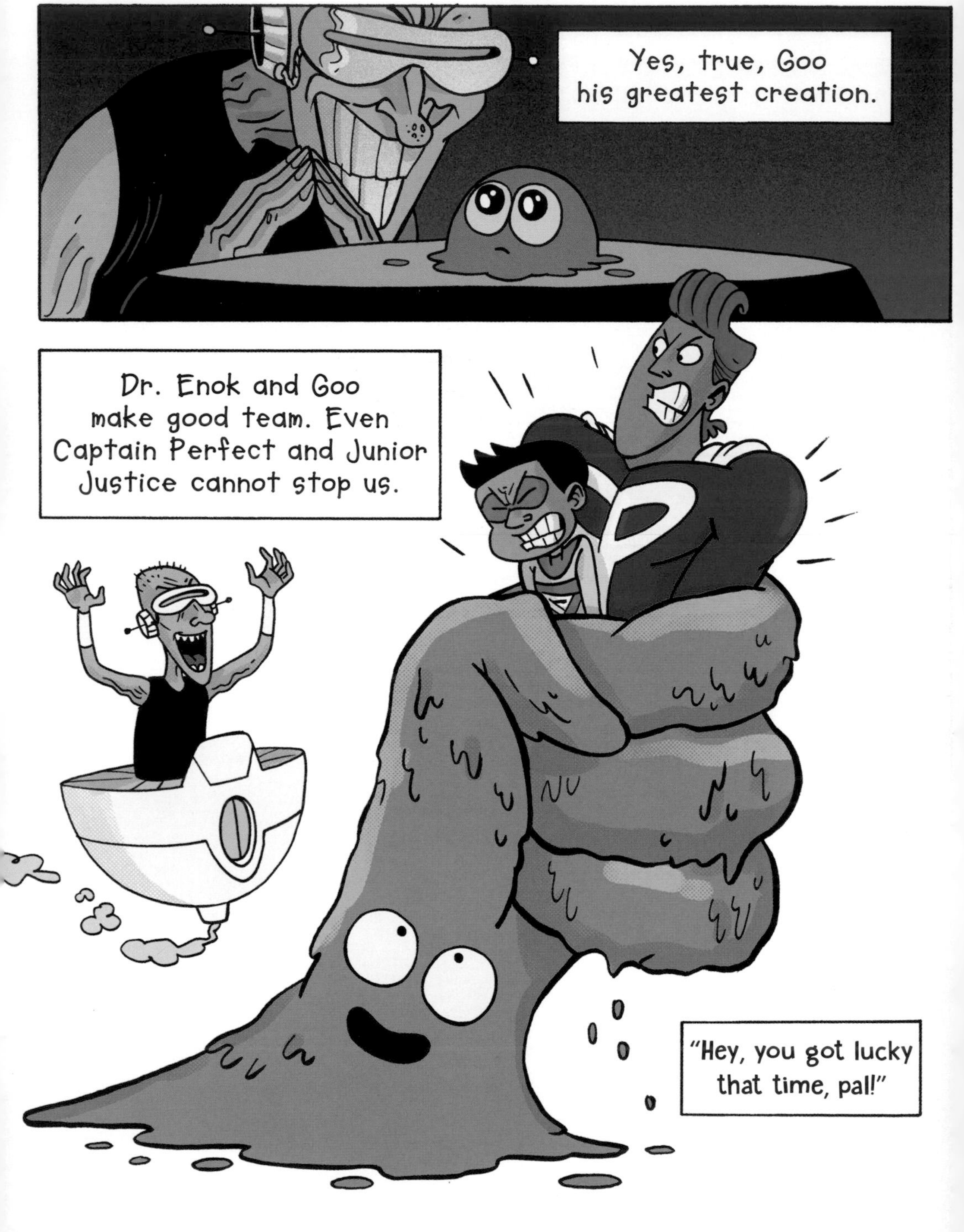
Yes, true, Goo
his greatest creation.
Dr. Enok and Goo
make good team. Even
Captain Perfect and Junior
Justice cannot stop us.
"Hey, you got lucky
that time, pal!"

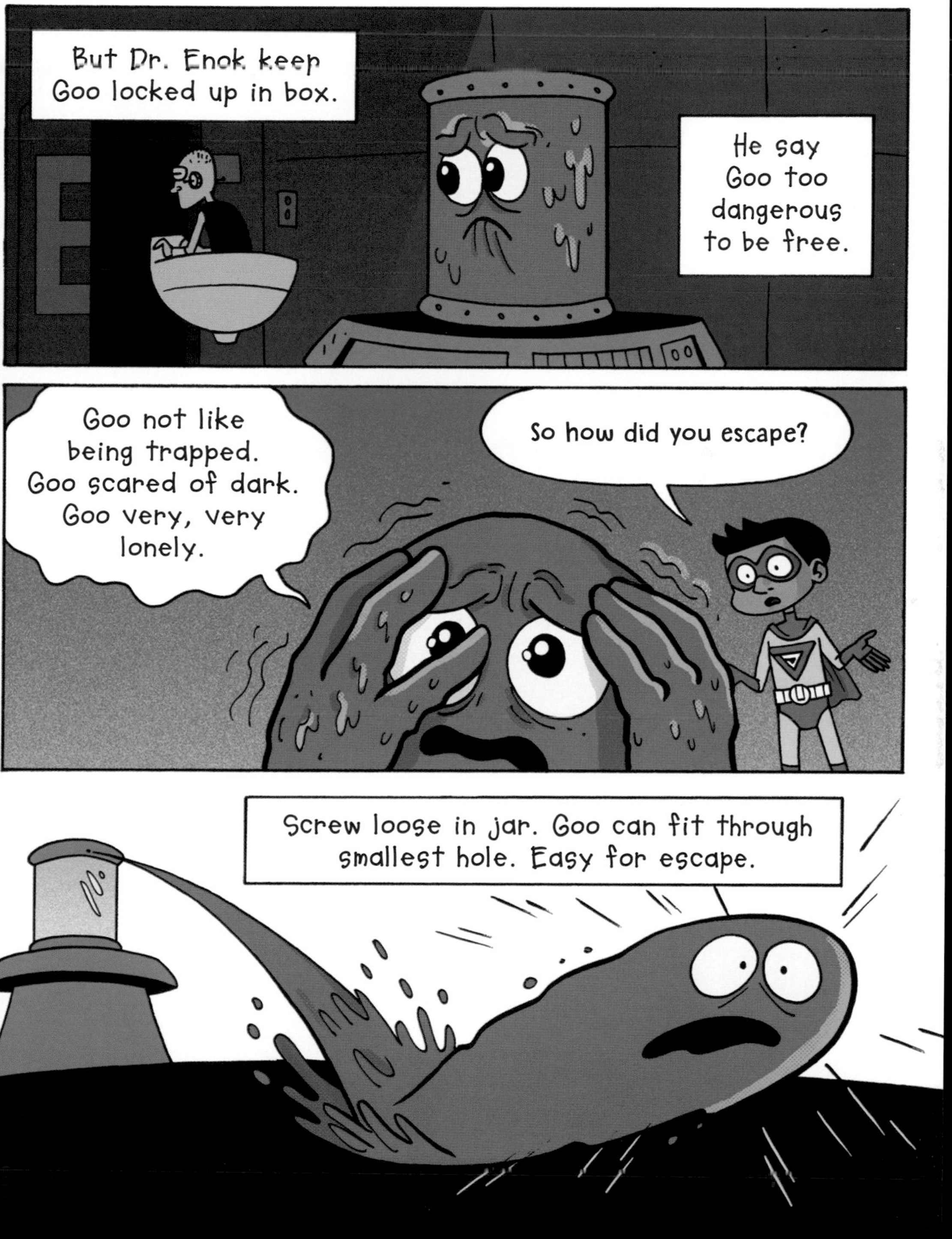
But Dr. Enok keep Goo locked up in box.
He say Goo too dangerous to be free.
Goo not like being trapped. Goo scared of dark. Goo very, very lonely.
So how did you escape?
Screw loose in jar. Goo can fit through smallest hole. Easy for escape.

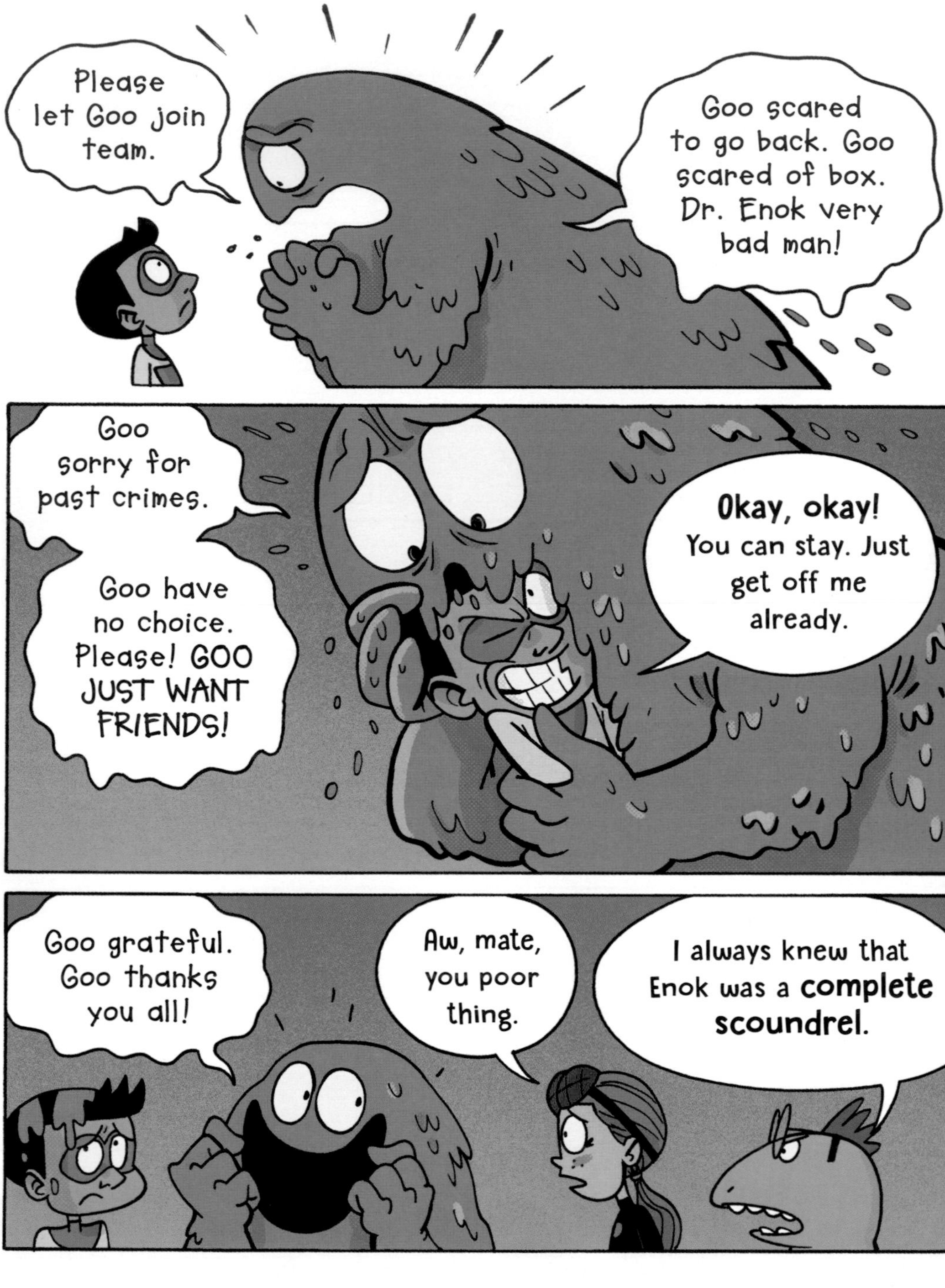

Please let Goo join team.
Goo scared to go back. Goo scared of box. Dr. Enok very bad man!
Goo sorry for past crimes.
Goo have no choice. Please! GOO JUST WANT FRIENDS!
Okay, okay! You can stay. Just get off me already.
Goo grateful. Goo thanks you all!
Aw, mate, you poor thing.
I always knew that Enok was a complete scoundrel.

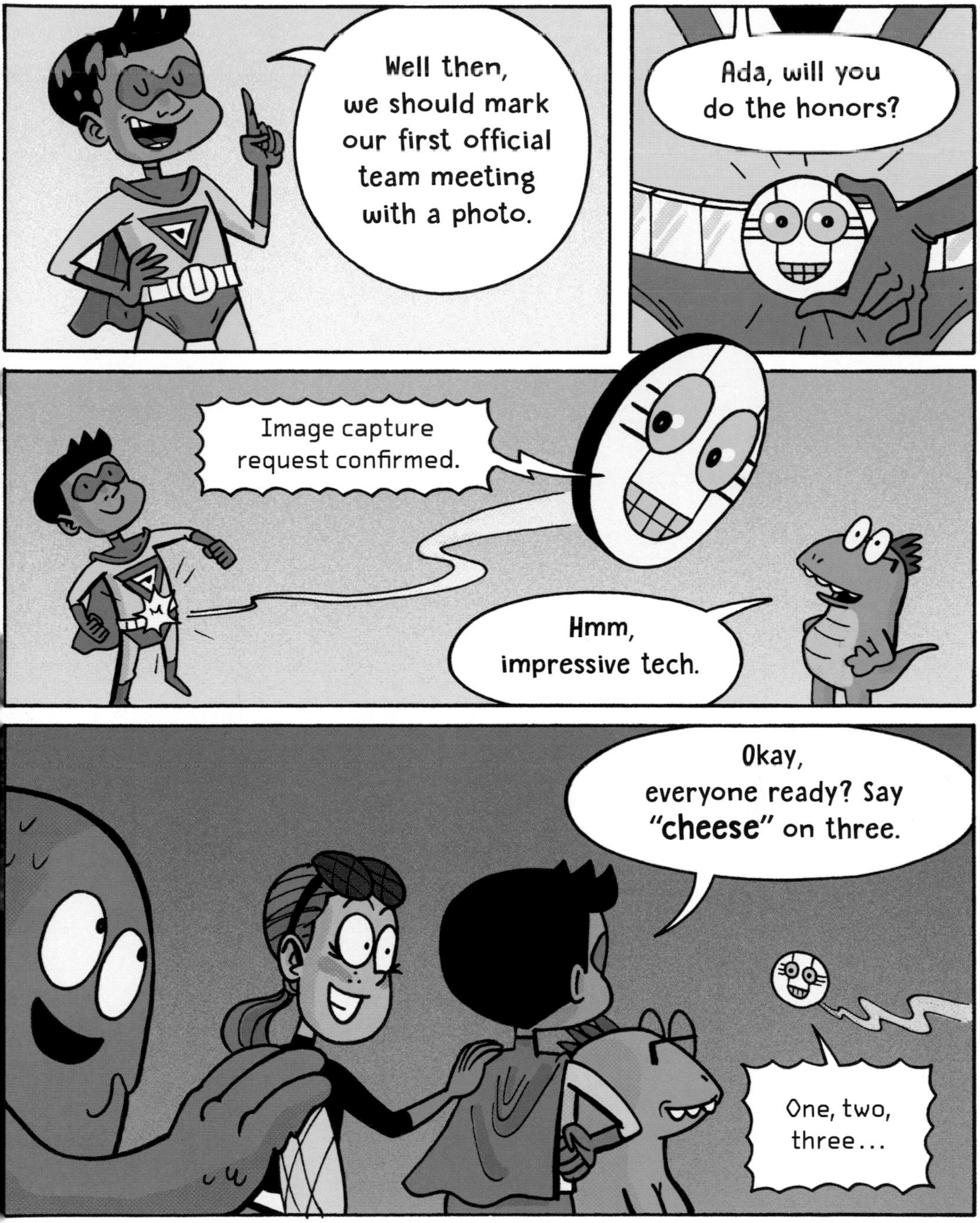
Well then, we should mark our first official team meeting with a photo.
Ada, will you do the honors?
Image capture request confirmed.
Hmm, impressive tech.
Okay, everyone ready? Say "cheese" on three.
One, two, three...

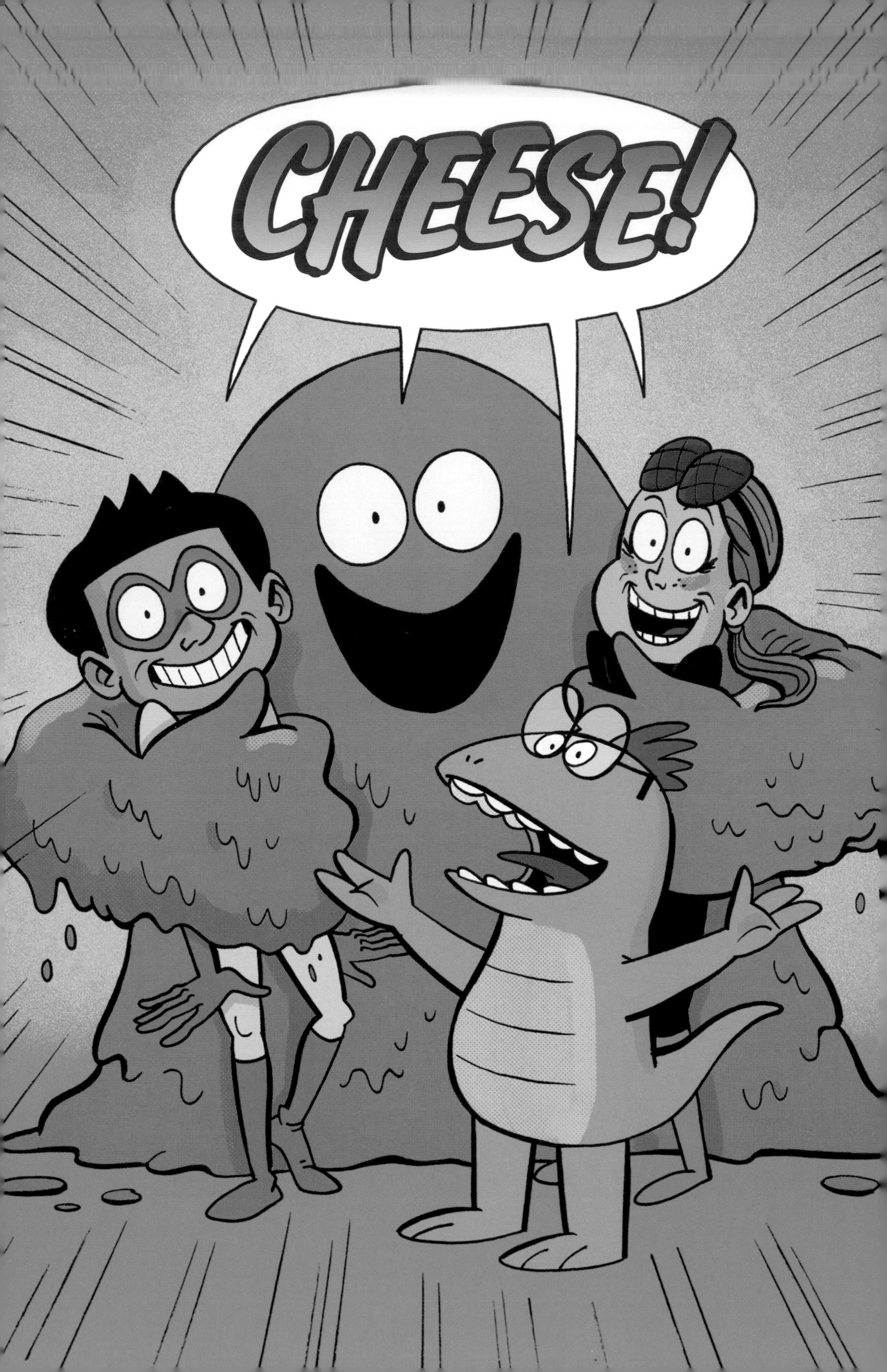
CHEESE!

Chapter

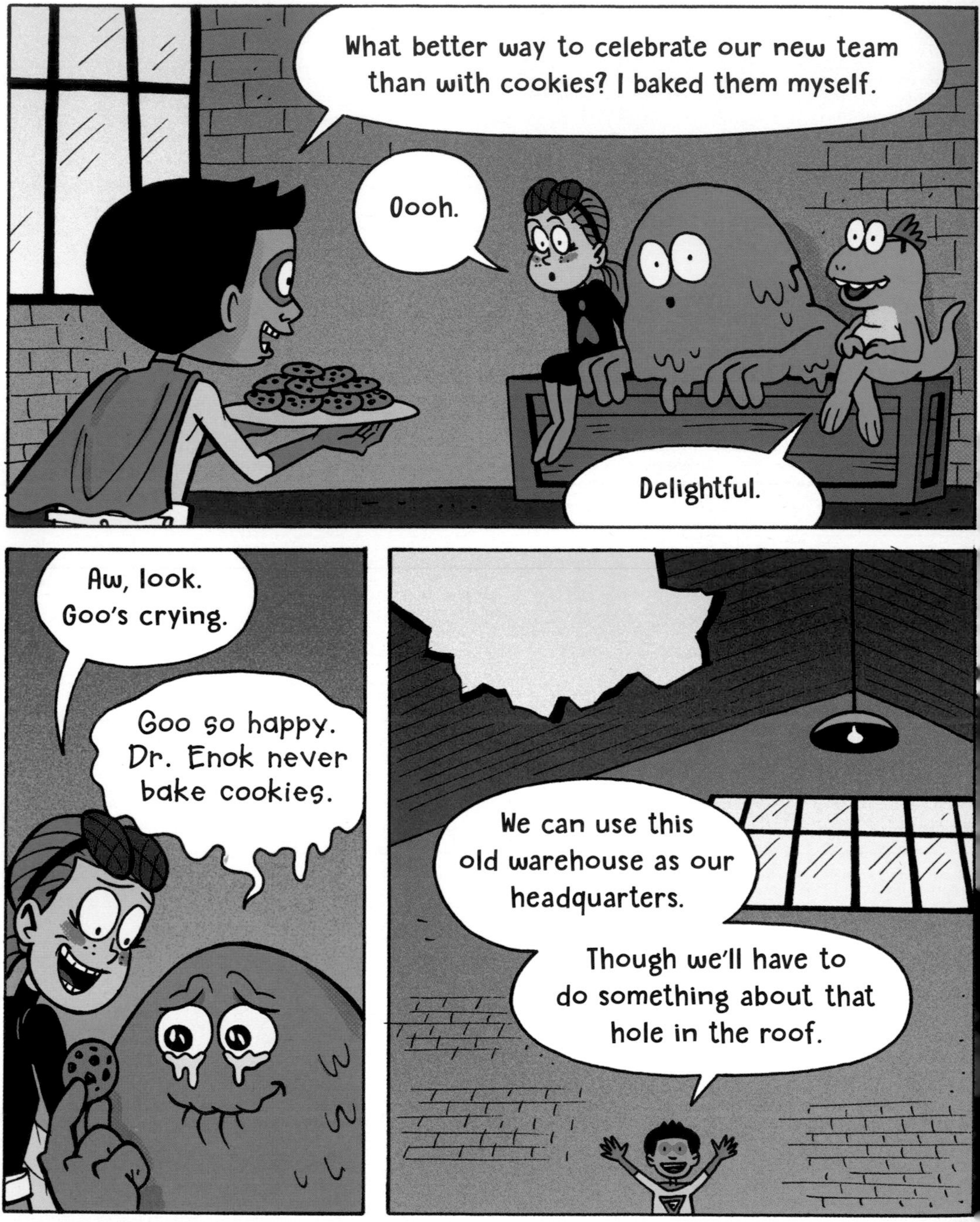
What better way to celebrate our new team than with cookies? I baked them myself.
Oooh.
Delightful.
Aw, look. Goo's crying.
Goo so happy. Dr. Enok never bake cookies.
We can use this old warehouse as our headquarters.
Though we'll have to do something about that hole in the roof.

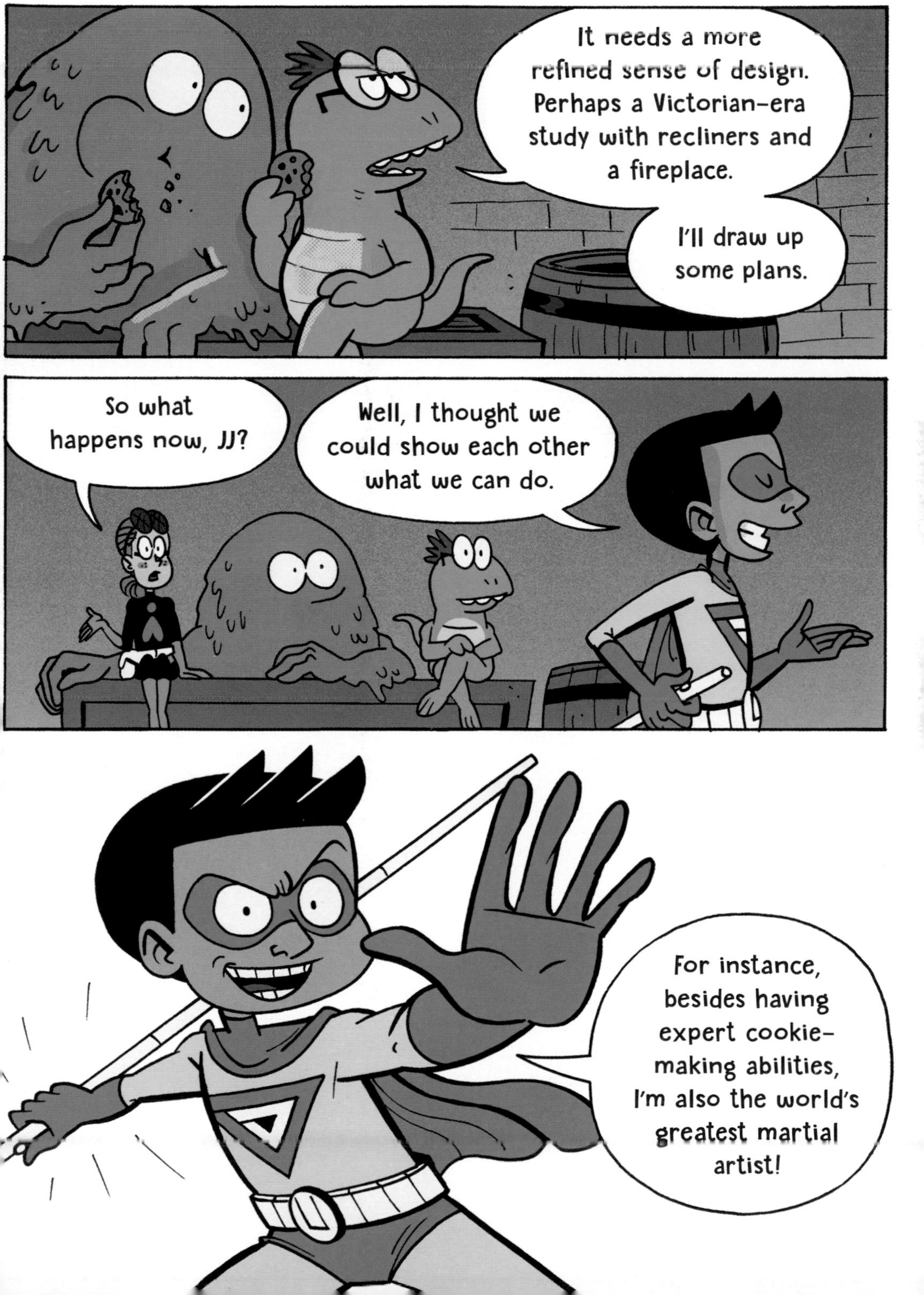
It needs a more refined sense of design. Perhaps a Victorian-era study with recliners and a fireplace.
I'll draw up some plans.
So what happens now, JJ?
Well, I thought we could show each other what we can do.
For instance, besides having expert cookie-making abilities, I'm also the world's greatest martial artist!

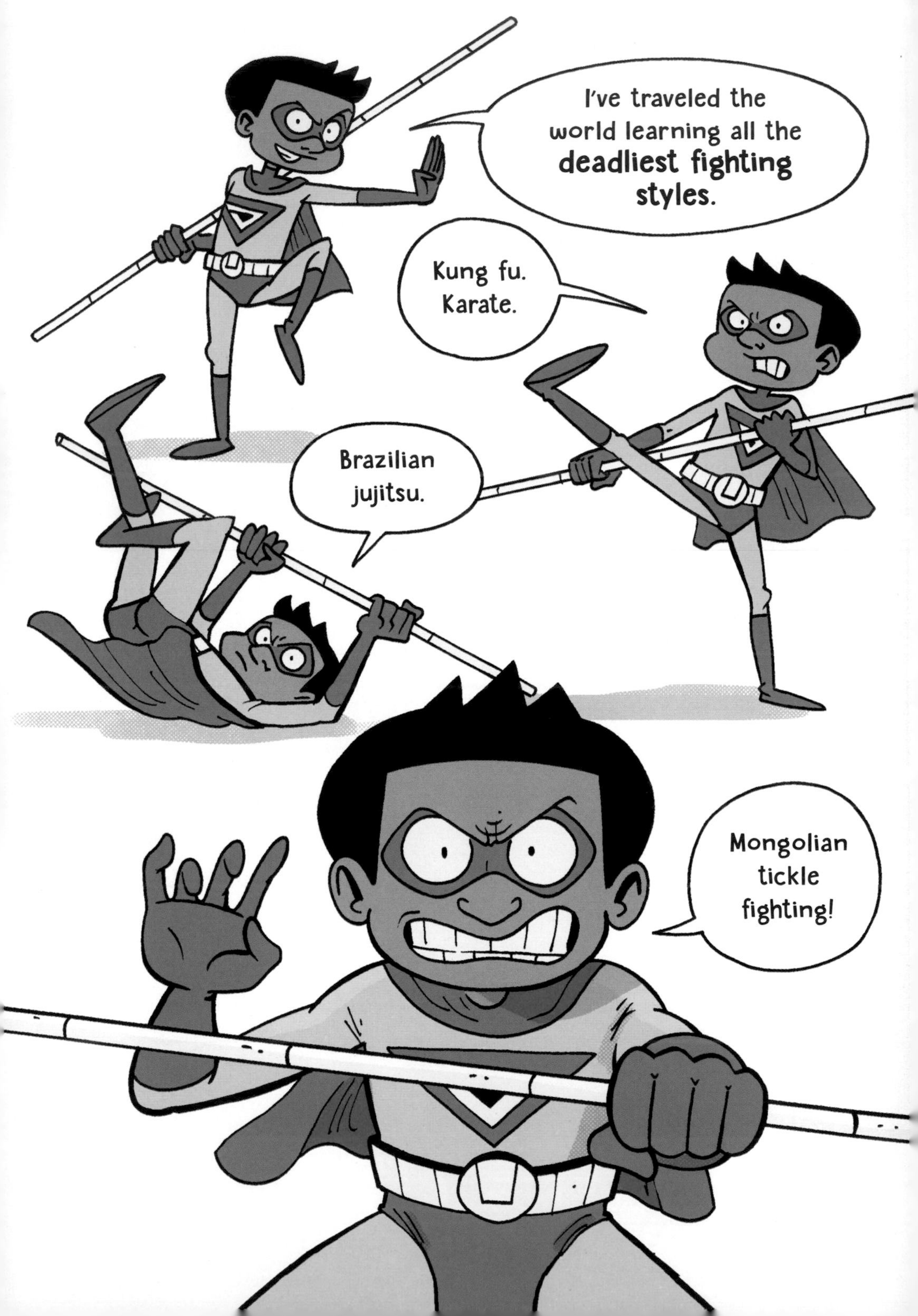
I've traveled the world learning all the **deadliest fighting styles.**
Kung fu. Karate.
Brazilian jujitsu.
Mongolian tickle fighting!

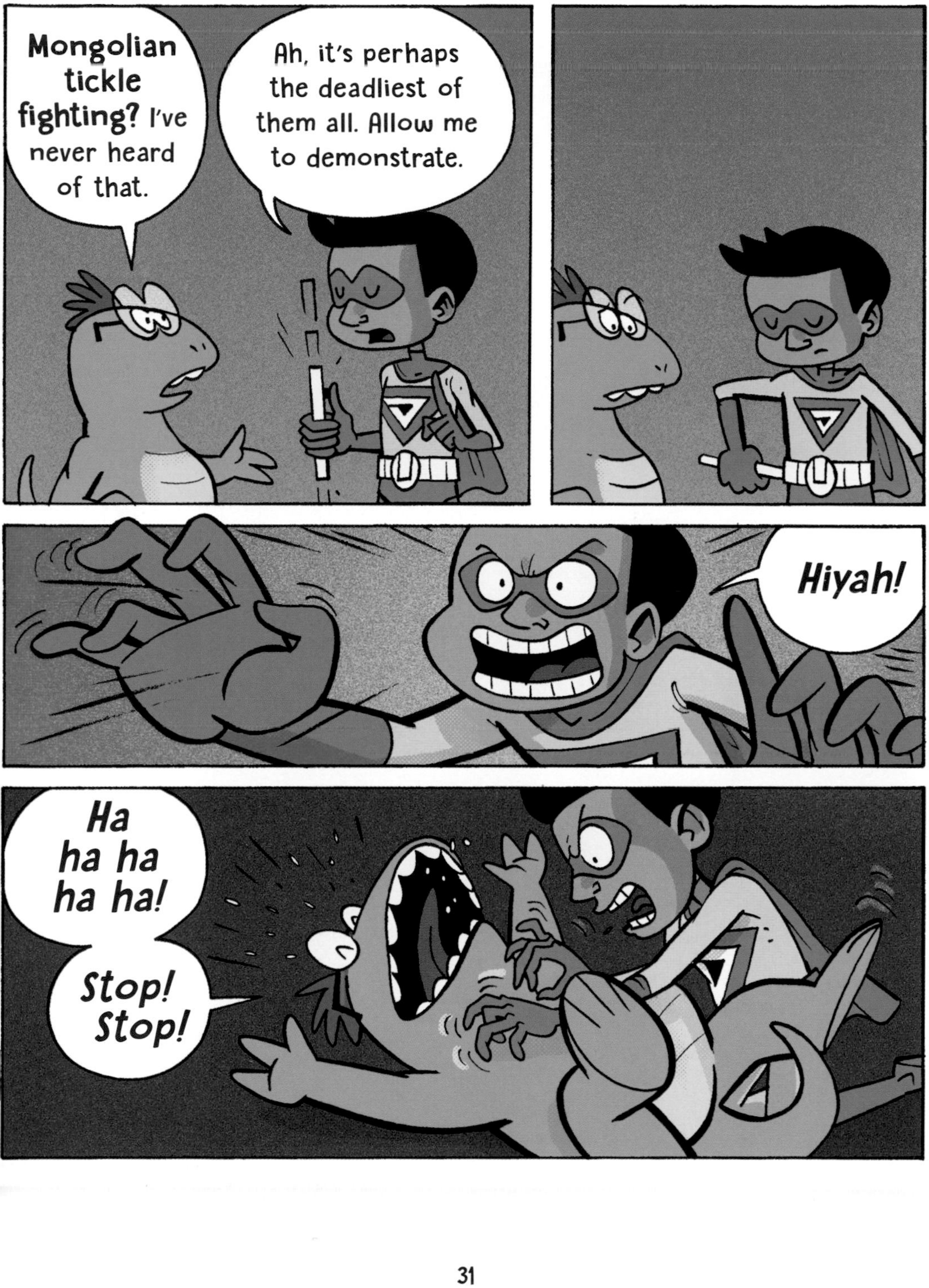

Mongolian tickle fighting? I've never heard of that.
Ah, it's perhaps the deadliest of them all. Allow me to demonstrate.
Hiyah!
Ha ha ha ha ha!
Stop! Stop!

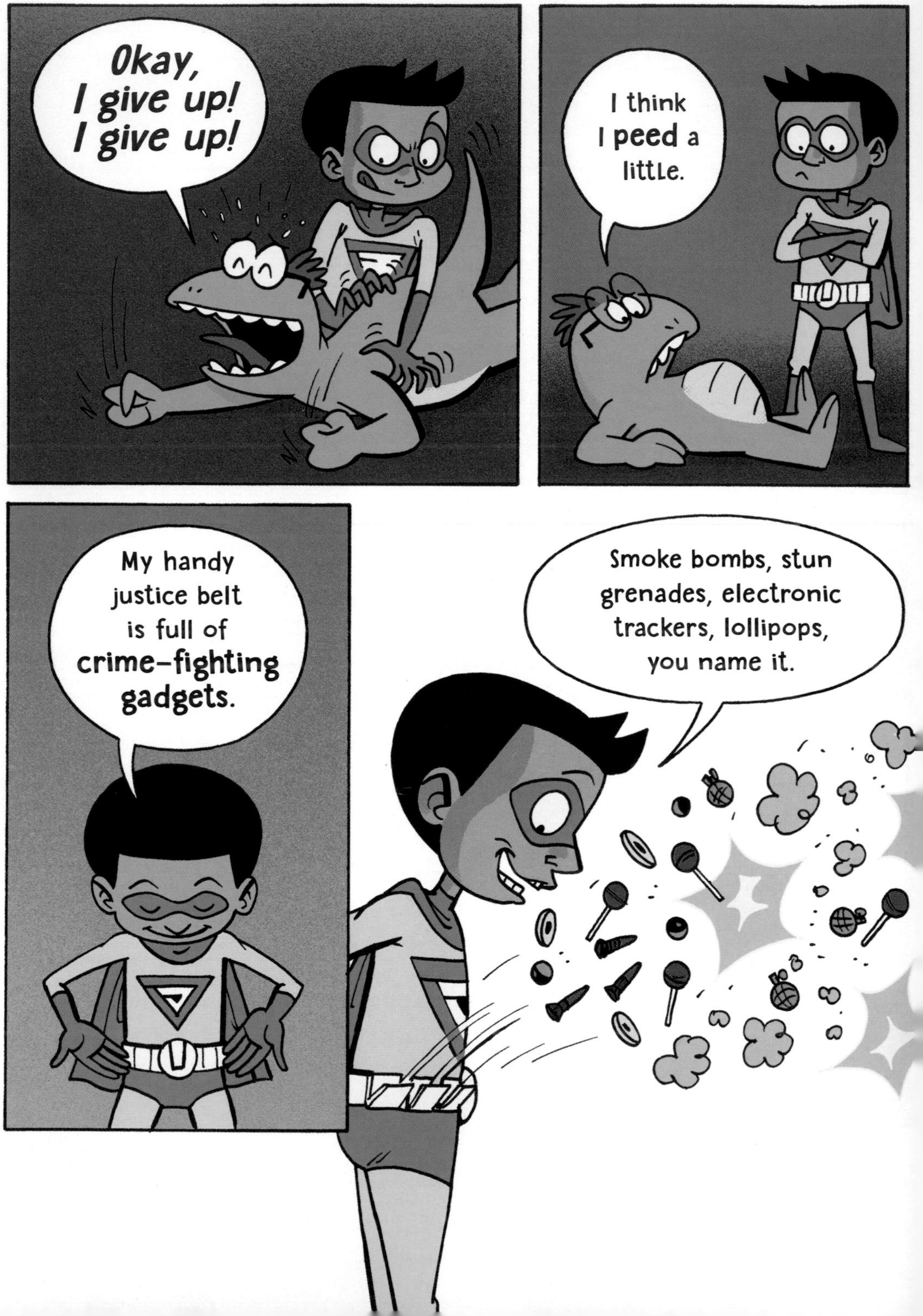
Okay, I give up! I give up!
I think I peed a little.
My handy justice belt is full of crime-fighting gadgets.
Smoke bombs, stun grenades, electronic trackers, lollipops, you name it.

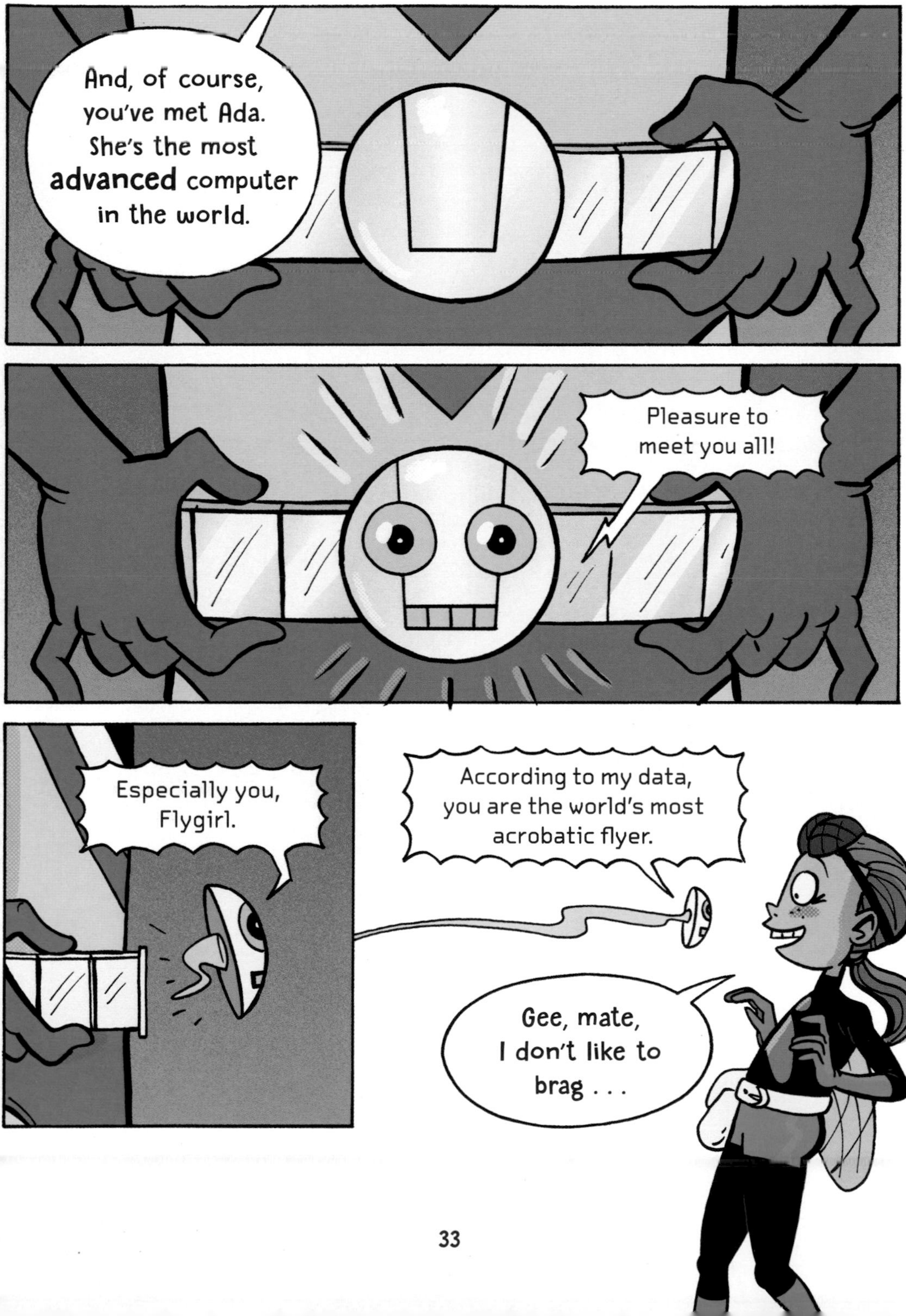
And, of course, you've met Ada. She's the most **advanced** computer in the world.
Pleasure to meet you all!
Especially you, Flygirl.
According to my data, you are the world's most acrobatic flyer.
Gee, mate, I don't like to brag . . .

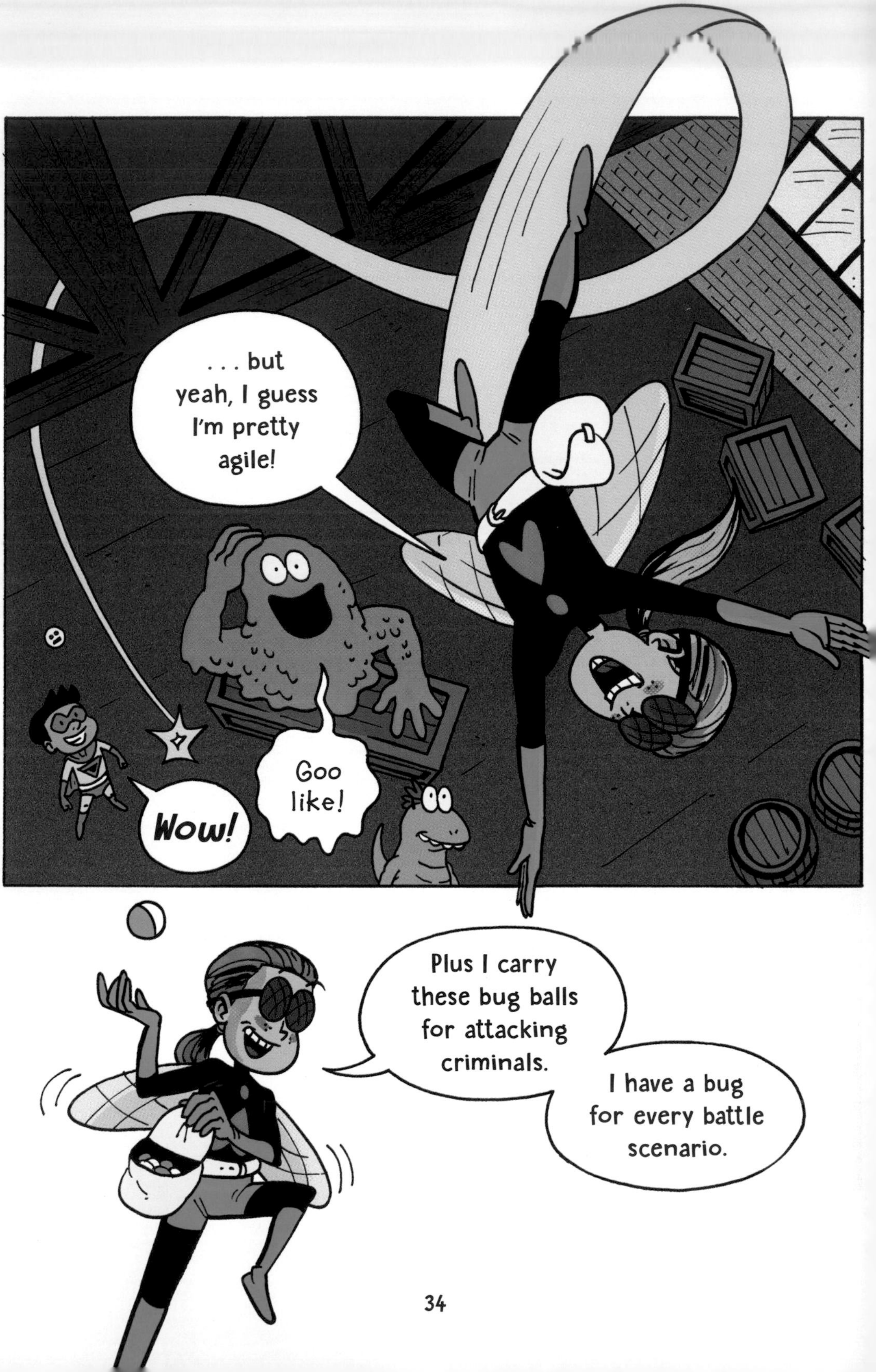
. . . but yeah, I guess I'm pretty agile!
Wow!
Goo like!
Plus I carry these bug balls for attacking criminals.
I have a bug for every battle scenario.

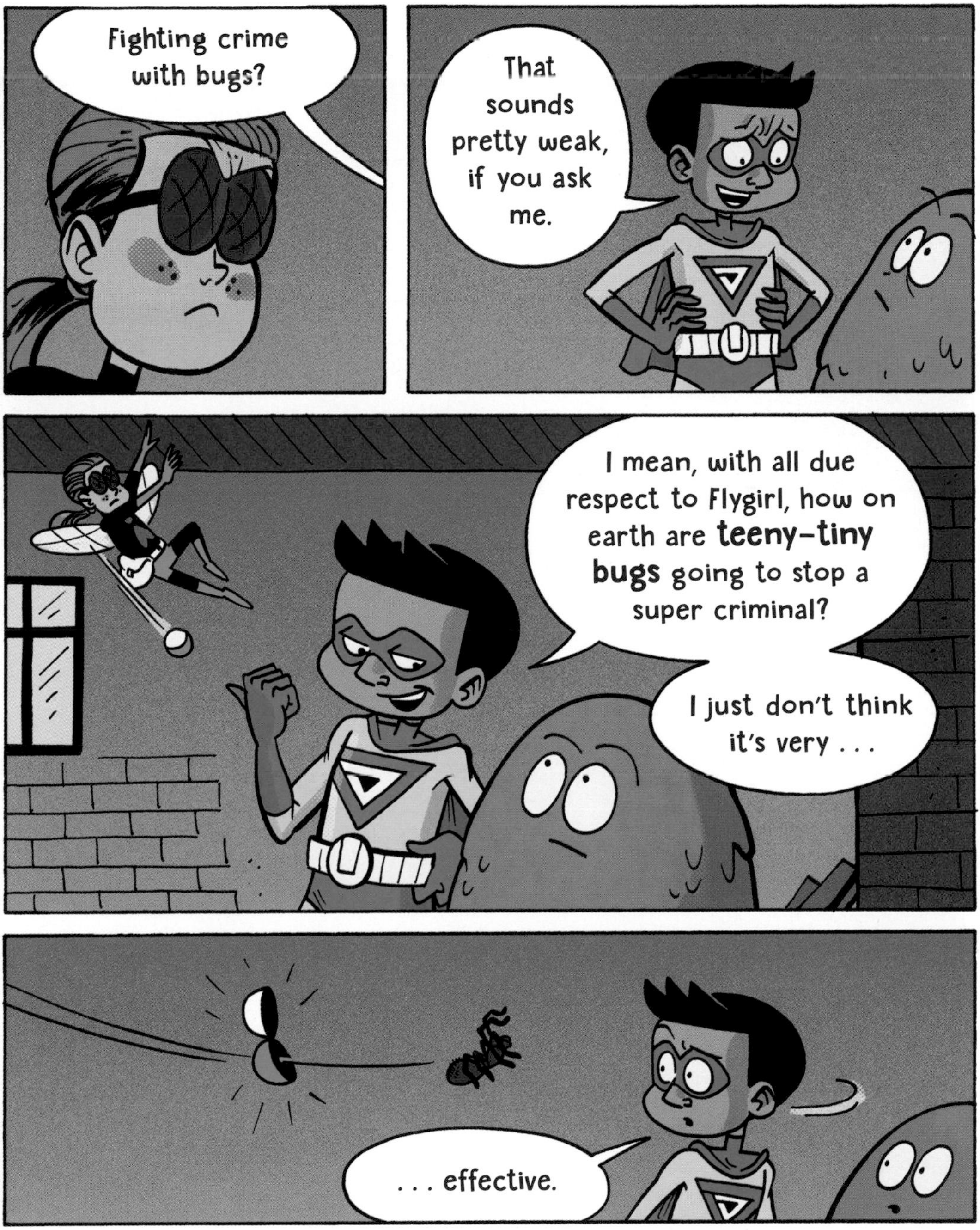
Fighting crime with bugs?
That sounds pretty weak, if you ask me.
I mean, with all due respect to Flygirl, how on earth are teeny-tiny bugs going to stop a super criminal?
I just don't think it's very . . .
. . . effective.

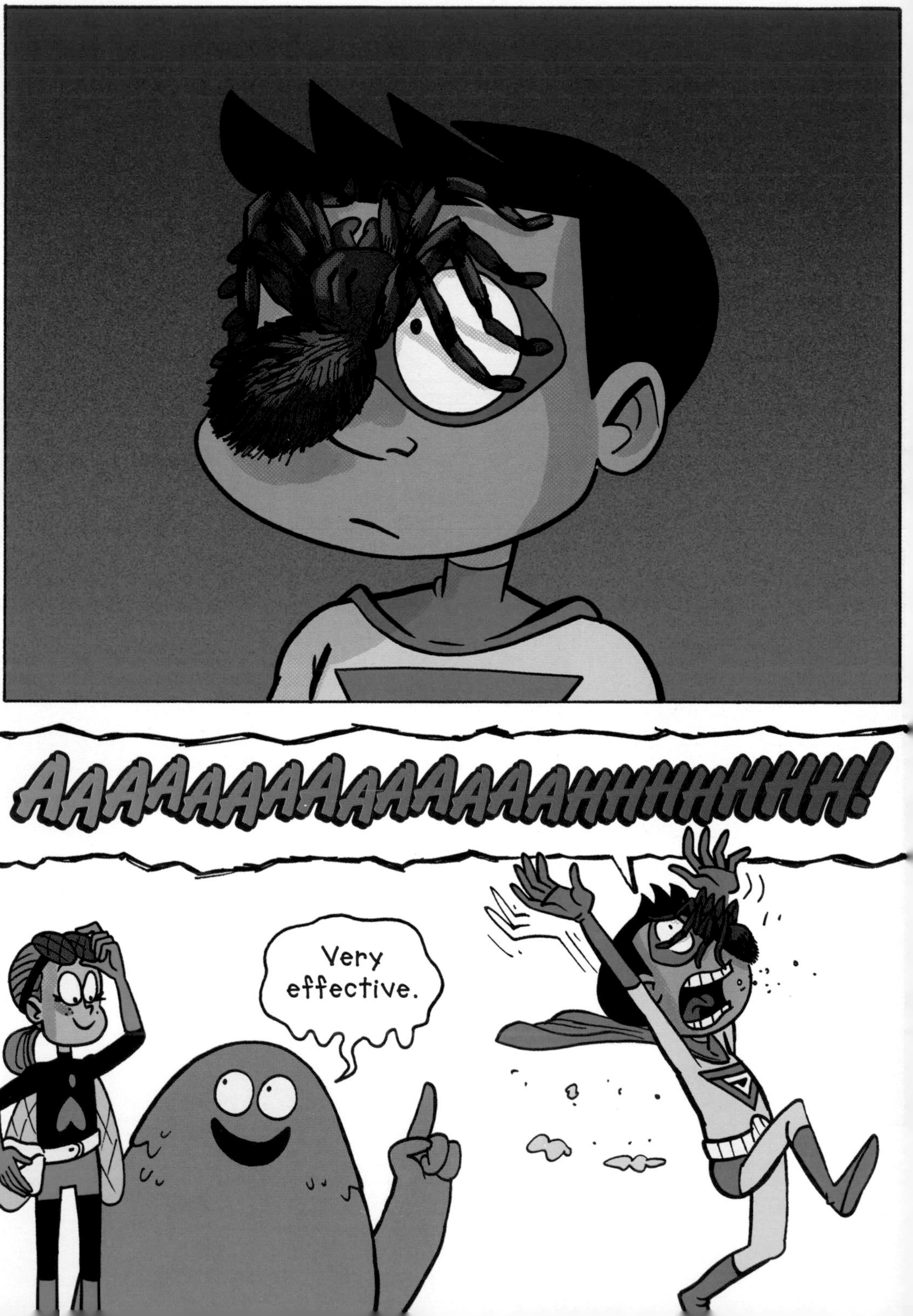
AAAAAAAAAAAAAAAAAHHHHHHHHH!
Very effective.

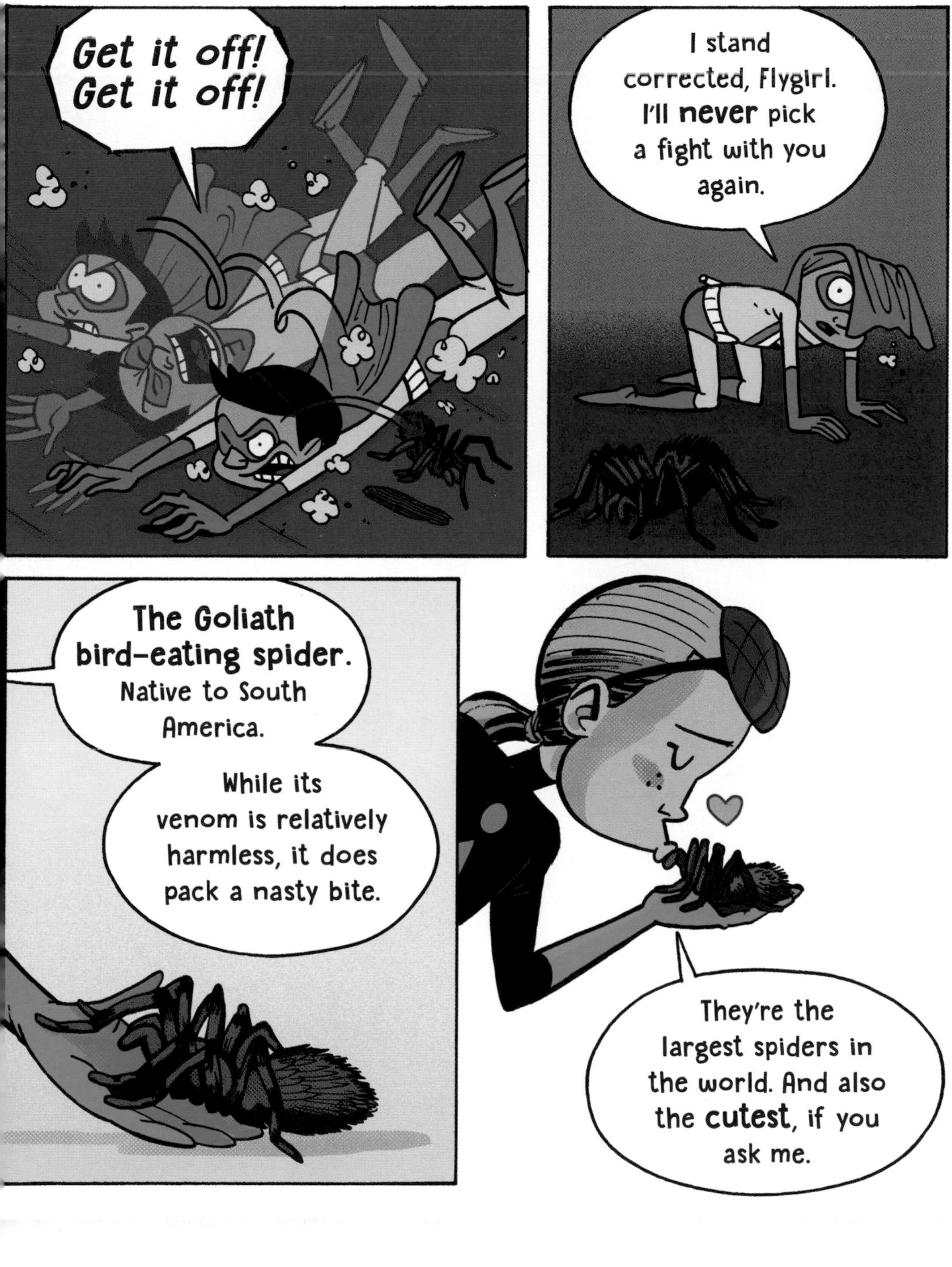
Get it off! Get it off!
I stand corrected, Flygirl. I'll **never** pick a fight with you again.
The Goliath bird-eating spider. Native to South America.
While its venom is relatively harmless, it does pack a nasty bite.
They're the largest spiders in the world. And also the **cutest**, if you ask me.

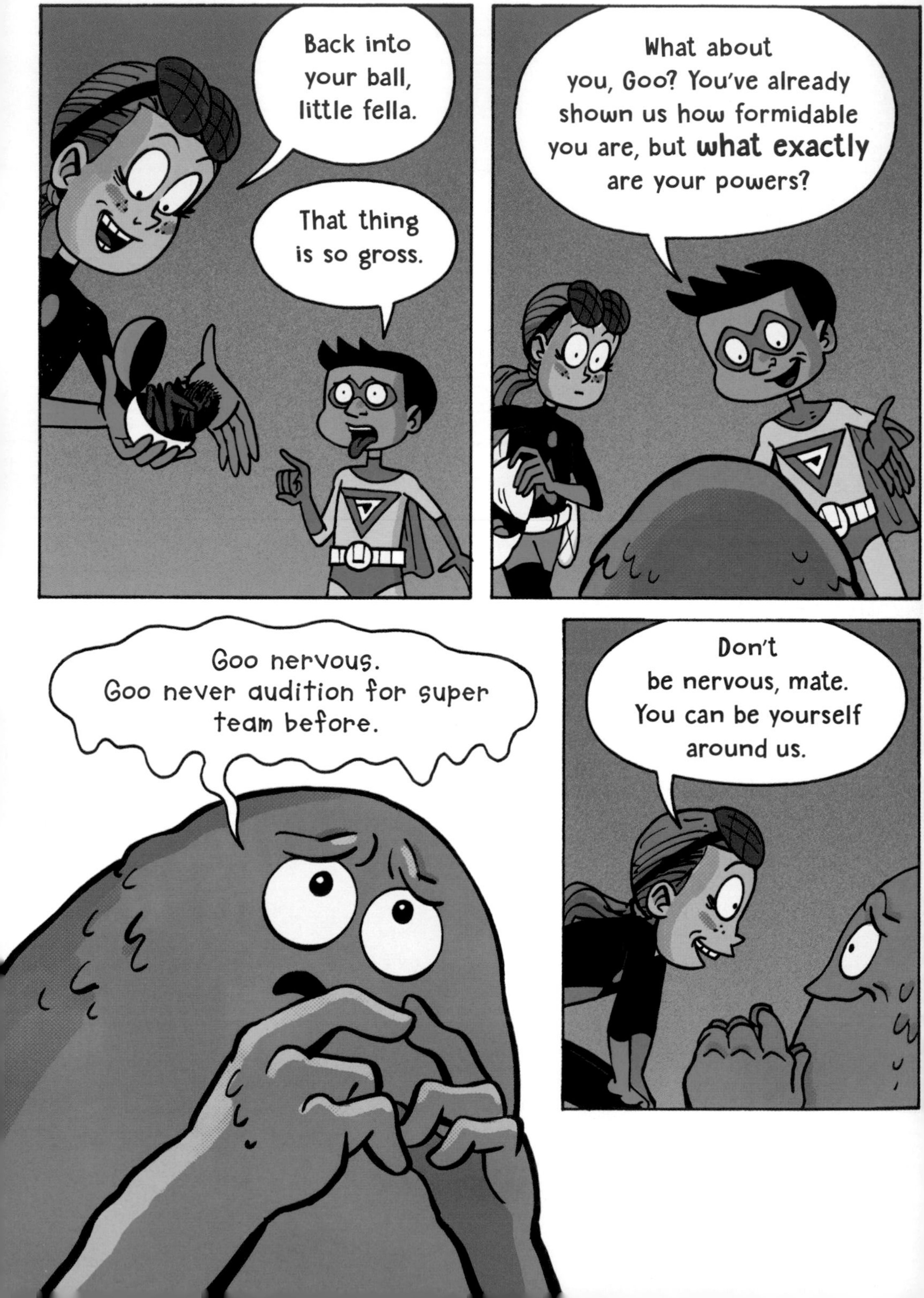
Back into your ball, little fella.
That thing is so gross.
What about you, Goo? You've already shown us how formidable you are, but **what exactly** are your powers?
Goo nervous. Goo never audition for super team before.
Don't be nervous, mate. You can be yourself around us.

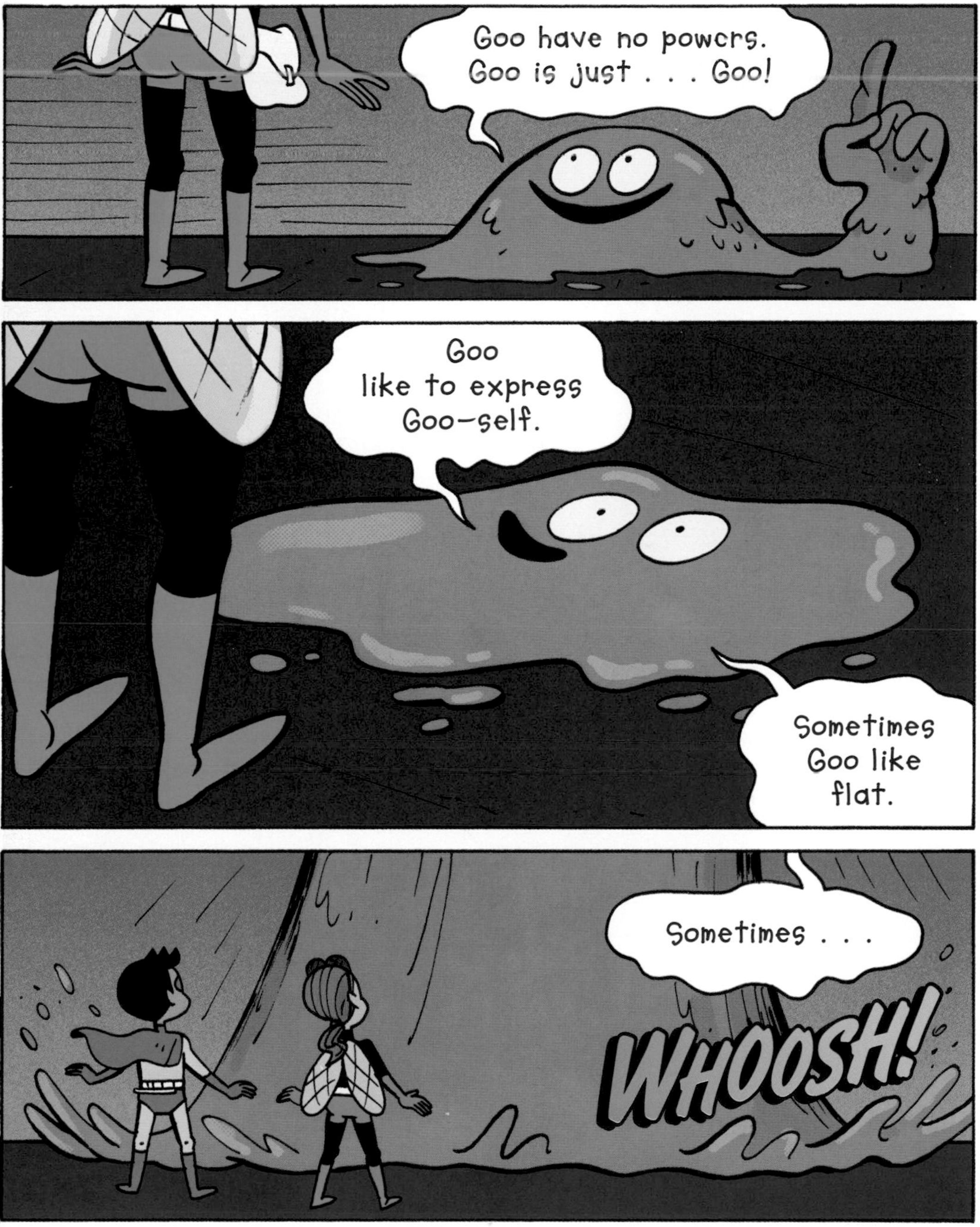
Goo have no powers. Goo is just . . . Goo!
Goo like to express Goo-self.
Sometimes Goo like flat.
Sometimes . . .
WHOOSH!

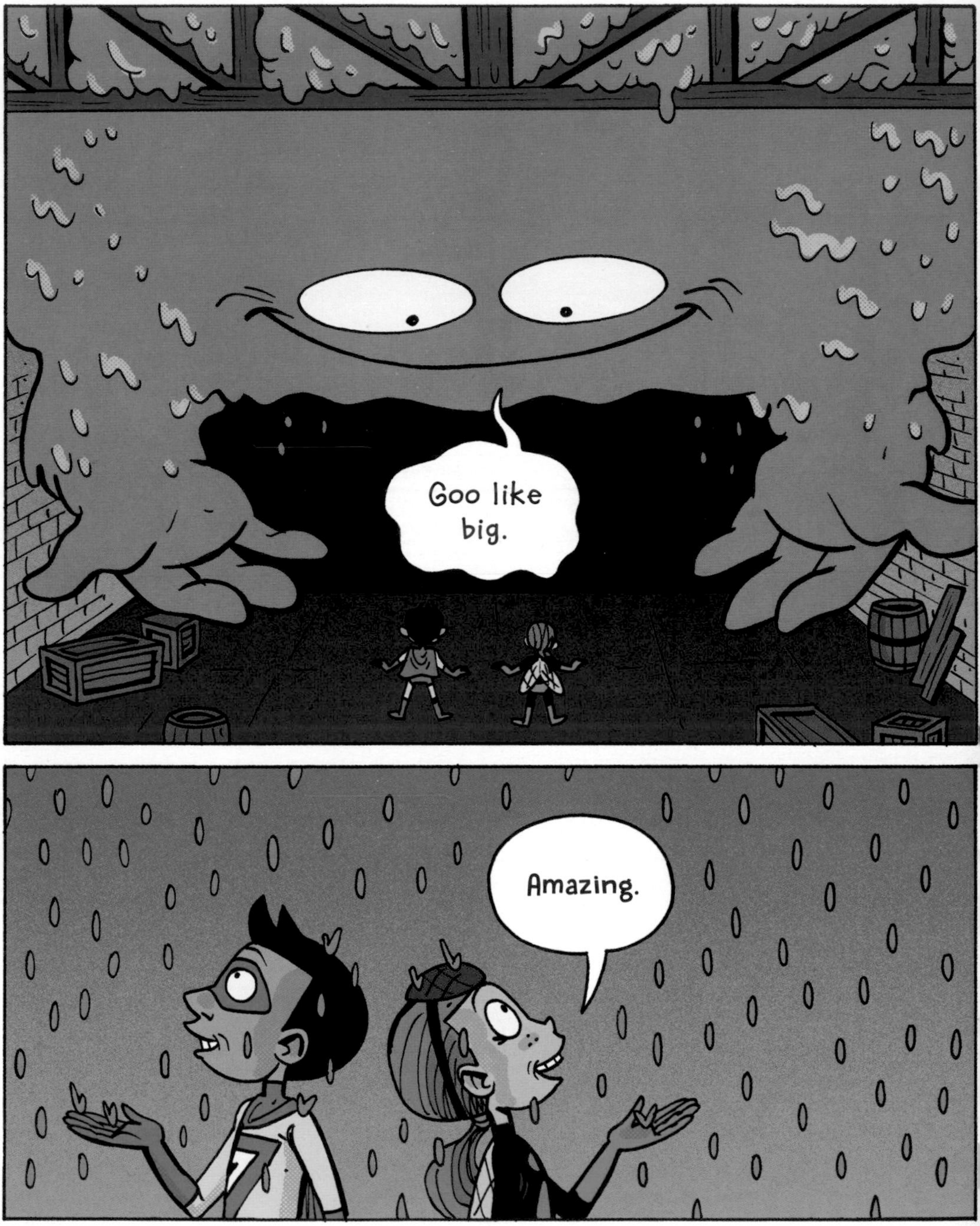
Goo like big.
Amazing.

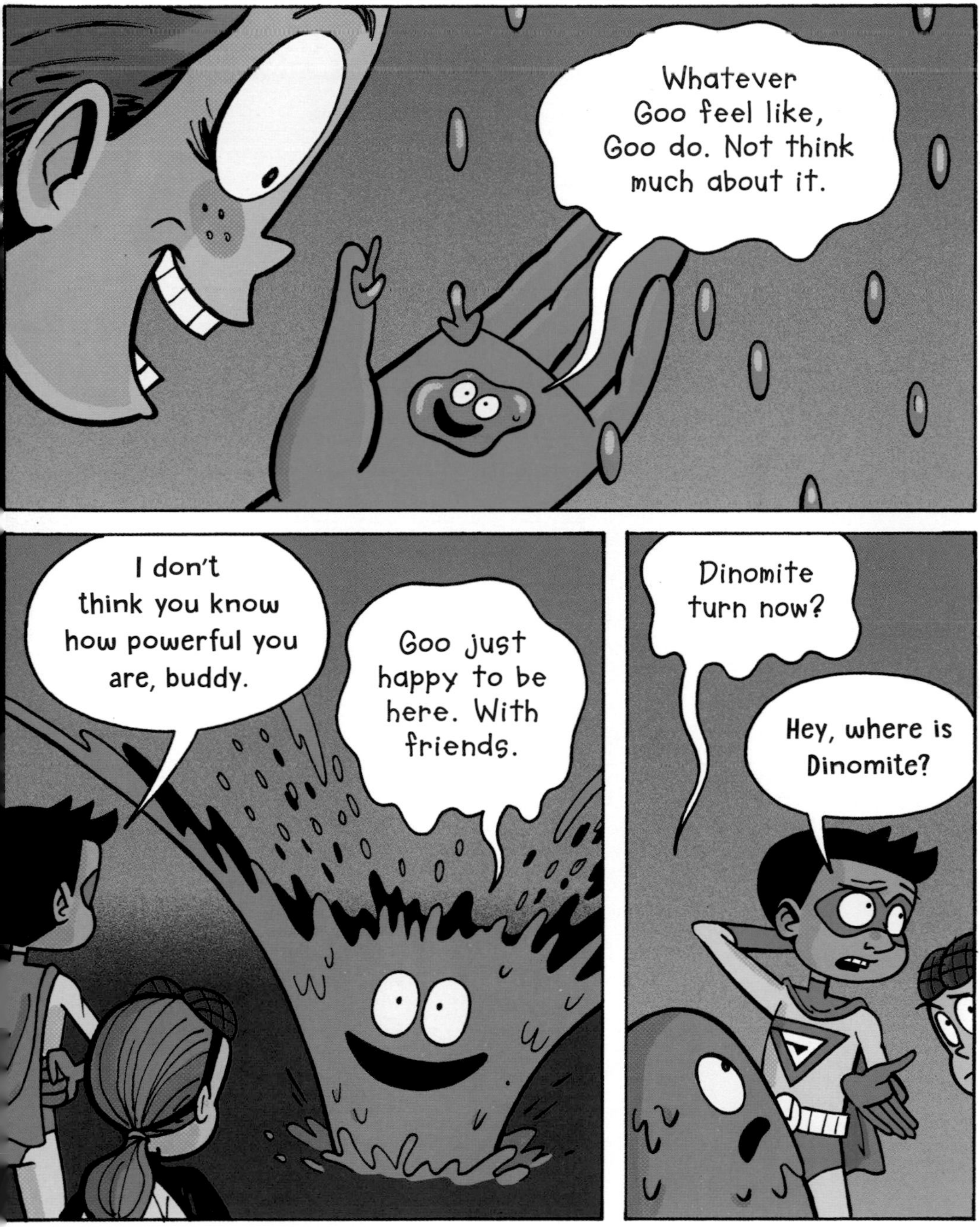
Whatever Goo feel like, Goo do. Not think much about it.
I don't think you know how powerful you are, buddy.
Goo just happy to be here. With friends.
Dinomite turn now?
Hey, where is Dinomite?

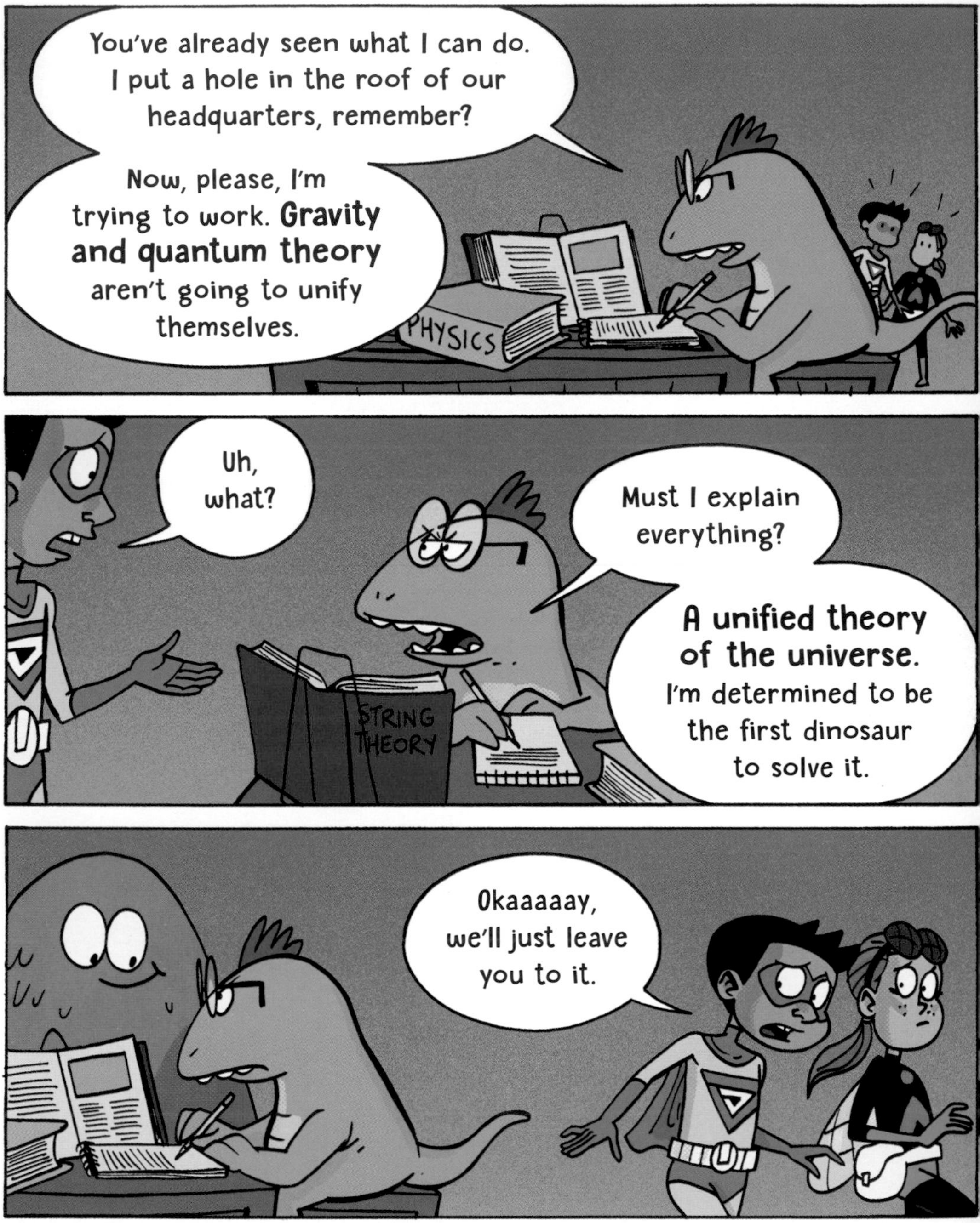
You've already seen what I can do. I put a hole in the roof of our headquarters, remember?
Now, please, I'm trying to work. **Gravity and quantum theory** aren't going to unify themselves.
PHYSICS
Uh, what?
Must I explain everything?
A unified theory of the universe. I'm determined to be the first dinosaur to solve it.
STRING THEORY
Okaaaaay, we'll just leave you to it.

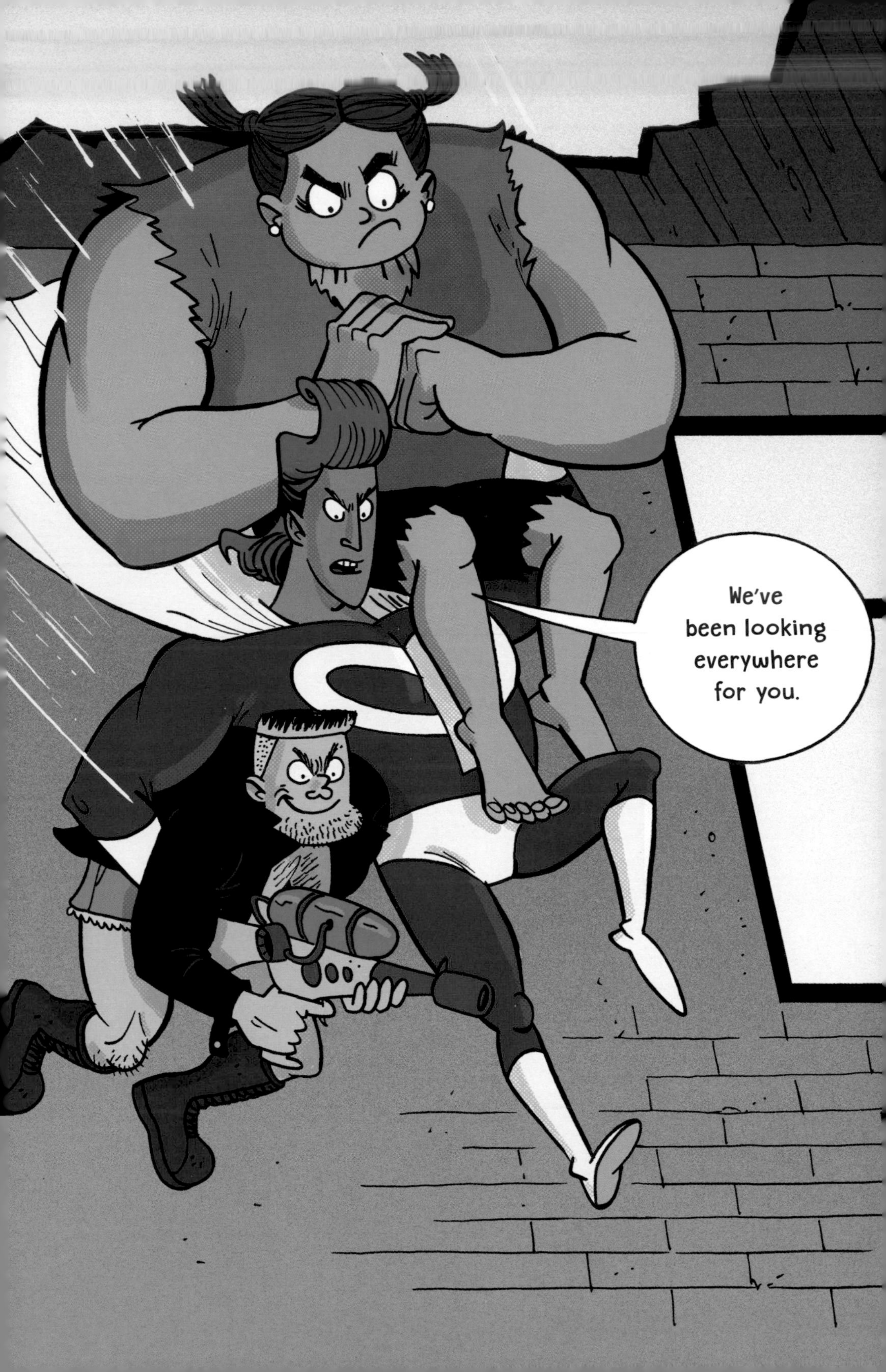
We've been looking everywhere for you.

Chapter

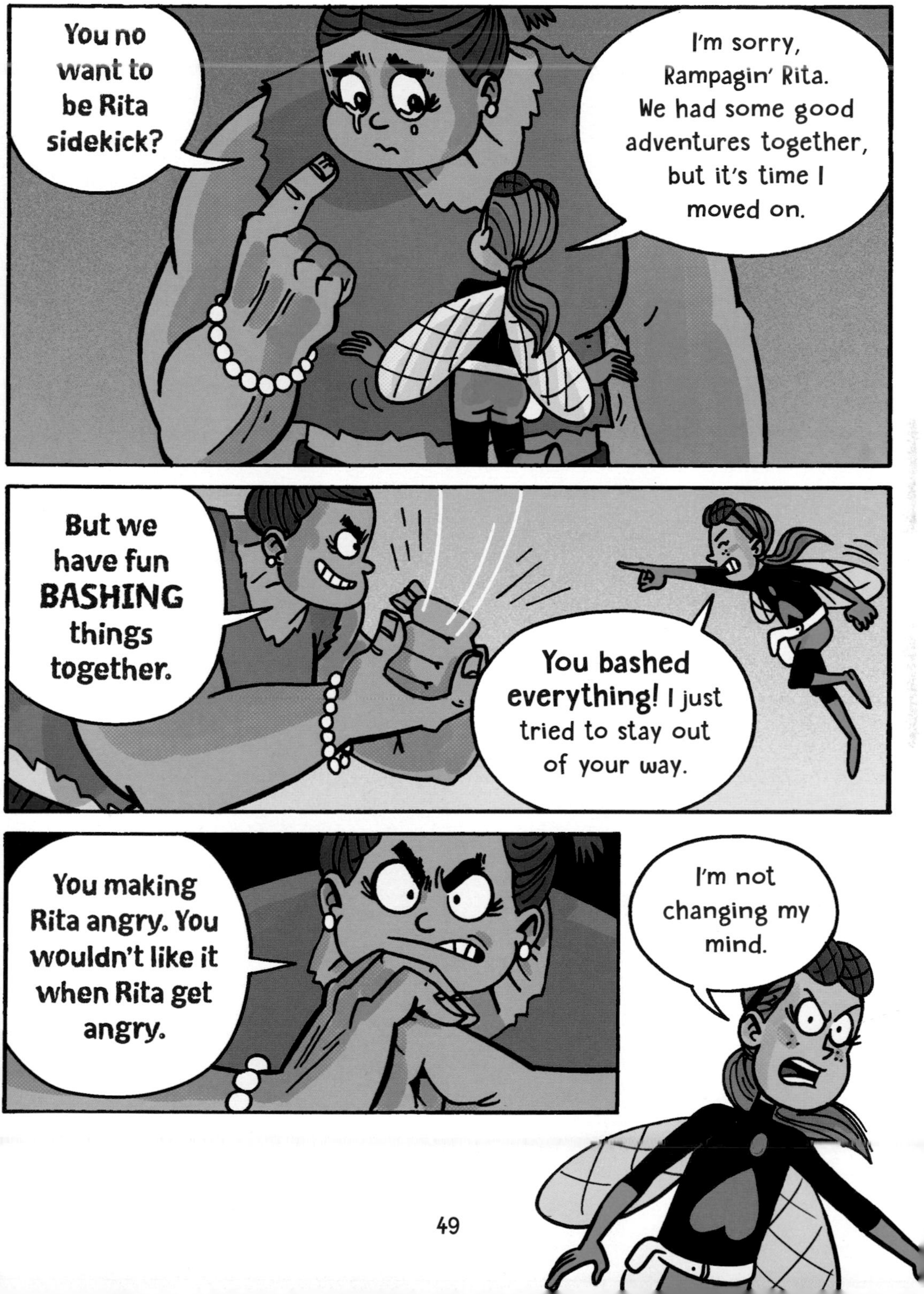
You no want to be Rita sidekick?
I'm sorry, Rampagin' Rita. We had some good adventures together, but it's time I moved on.
But we have fun BASHING things together.
You bashed everything! I just tried to stay out of your way.
You making Rita angry. You wouldn't like it when Rita get angry.
I'm not changing my mind.

Leave.

Night-night time.

Suddenly very sleepy . . .

FHOOF!

Dinomite!

He's out cold.

I have to say, my feelings are hurt.

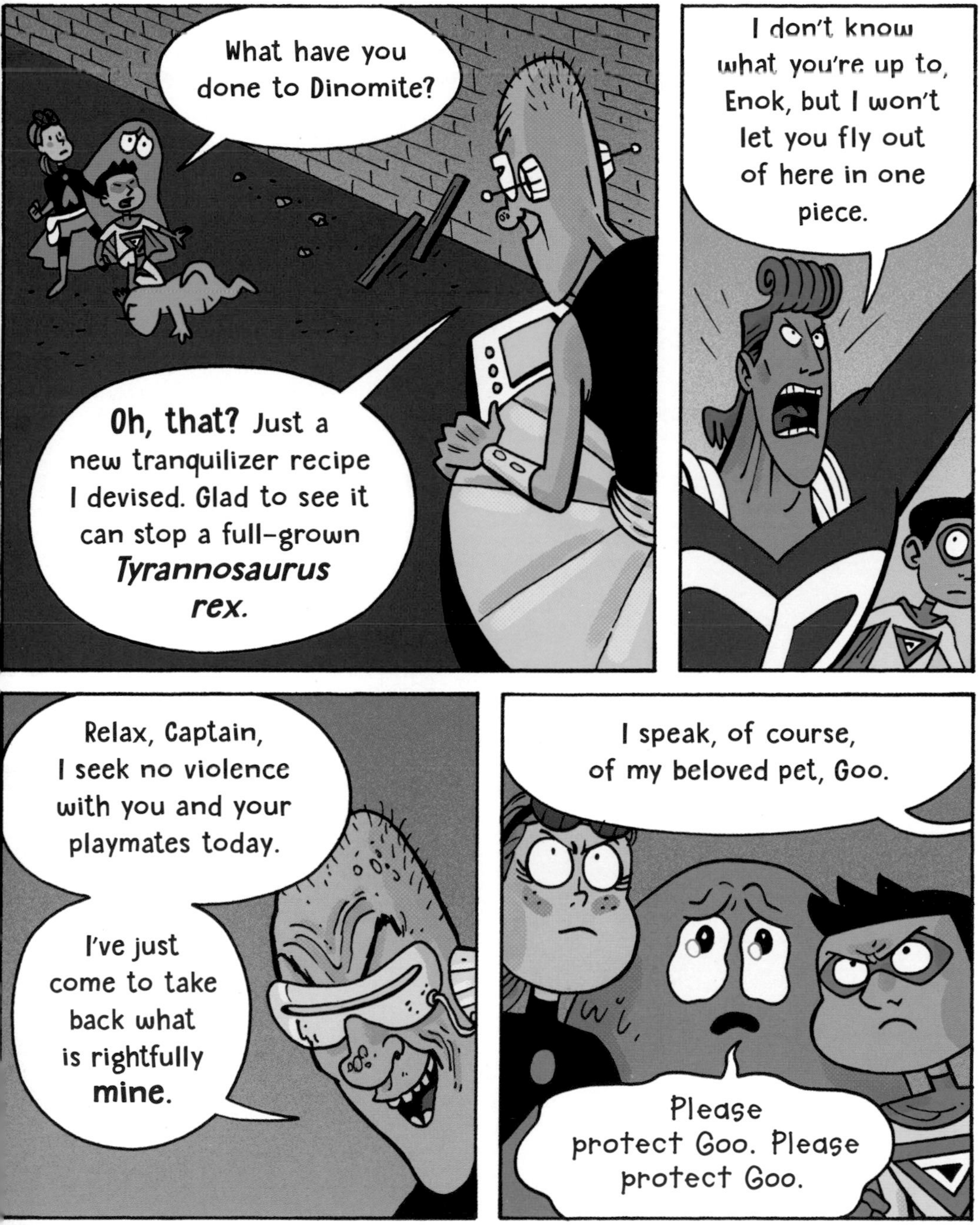
What have you done to Dinomite?
Oh, that? Just a new tranquilizer recipe I devised. Glad to see it can stop a full-grown *Tyrannosaurus rex*.
I don't know what you're up to, Enok, but I won't let you fly out of here in one piece.
Relax, Captain, I seek no violence with you and your playmates today.
I've just come to take back what is rightfully **mine**.
I speak, of course, of my beloved pet, Goo.
Please protect Goo. Please protect Goo.

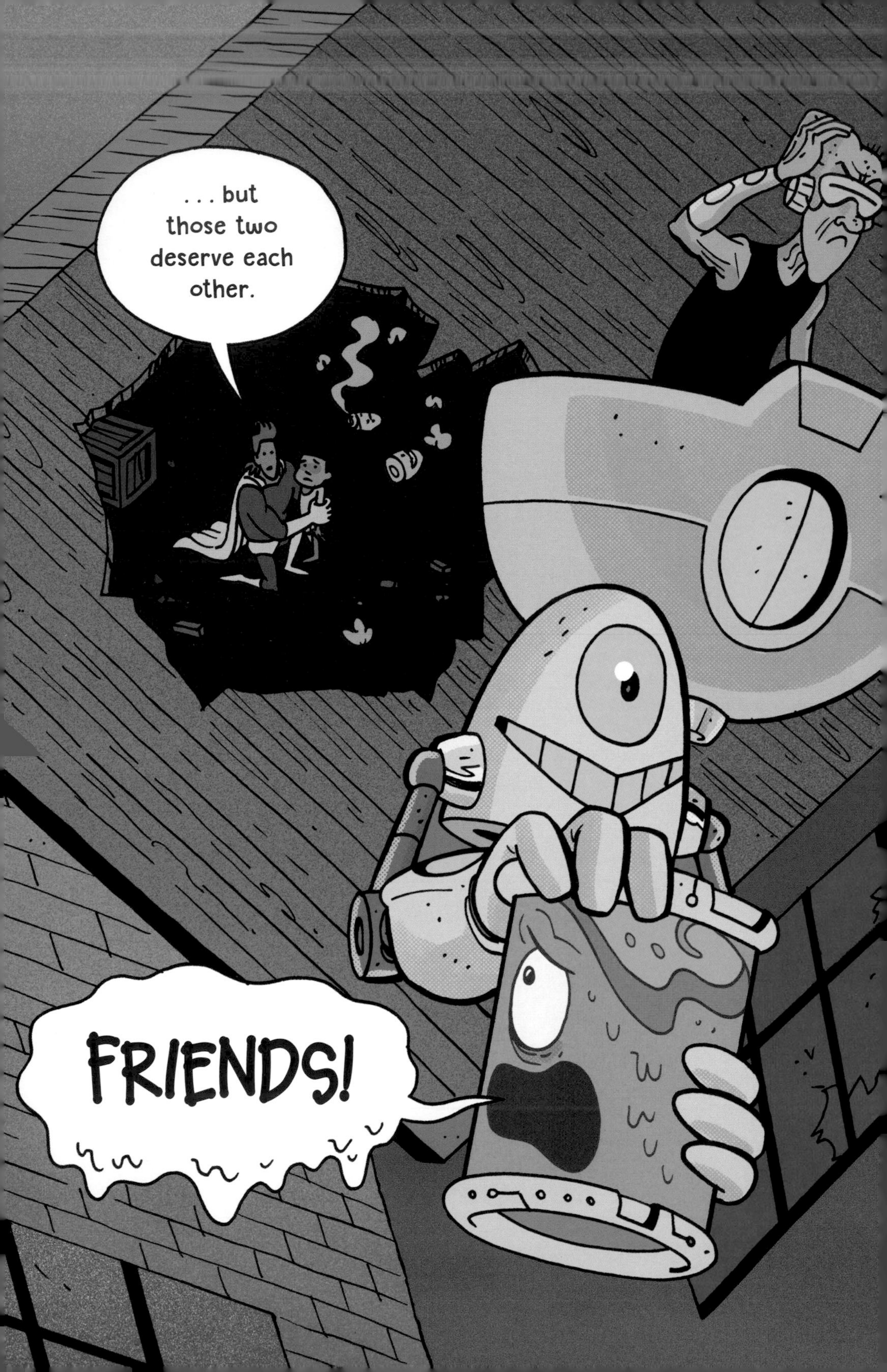
. . . but those two deserve each other.
FRIENDS!

Chapter

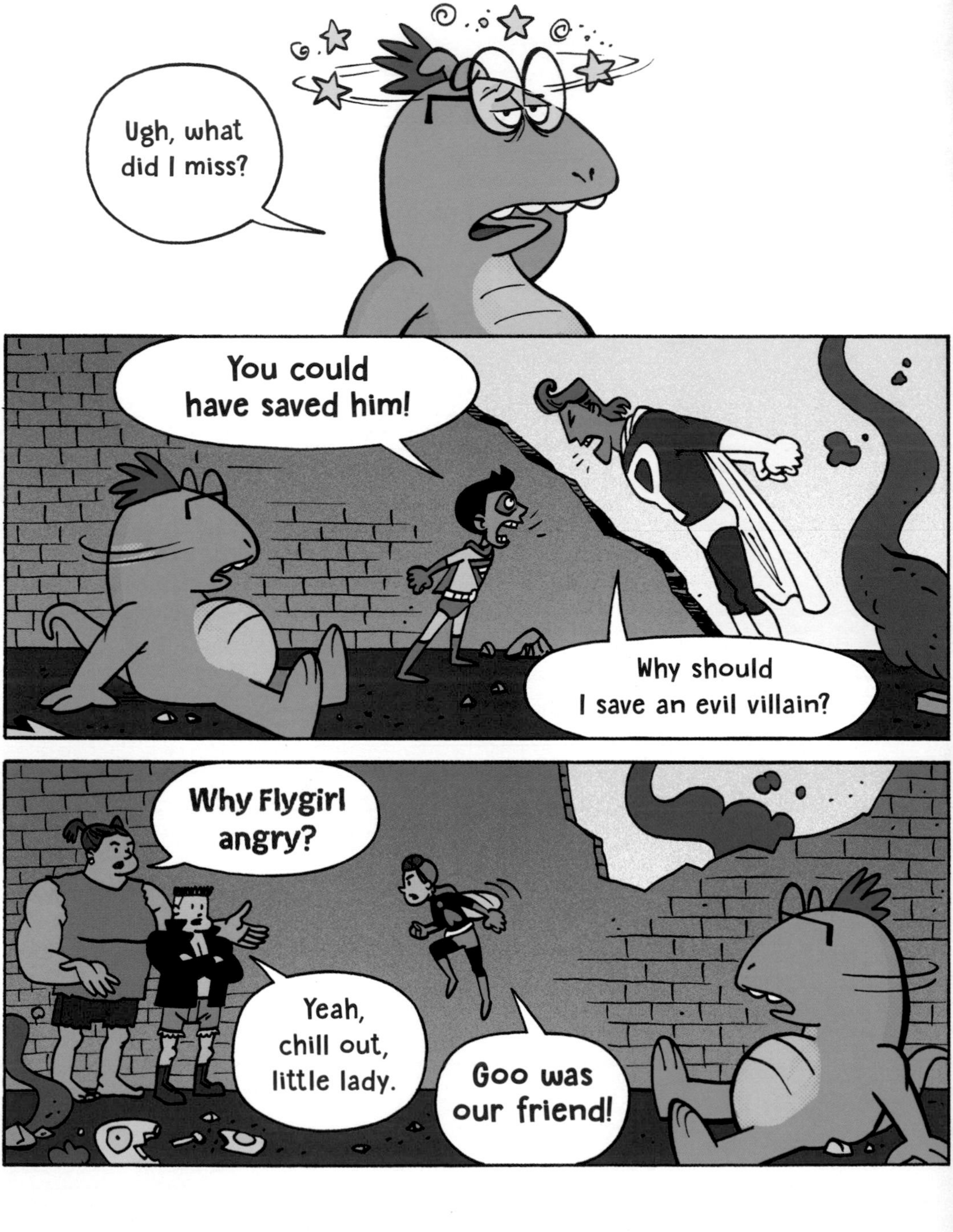
Ugh, what did I miss?
You could have saved him!
Why should I save an evil villain?
Why Flygirl angry?
Yeah, chill out, little lady.
Goo was our friend!

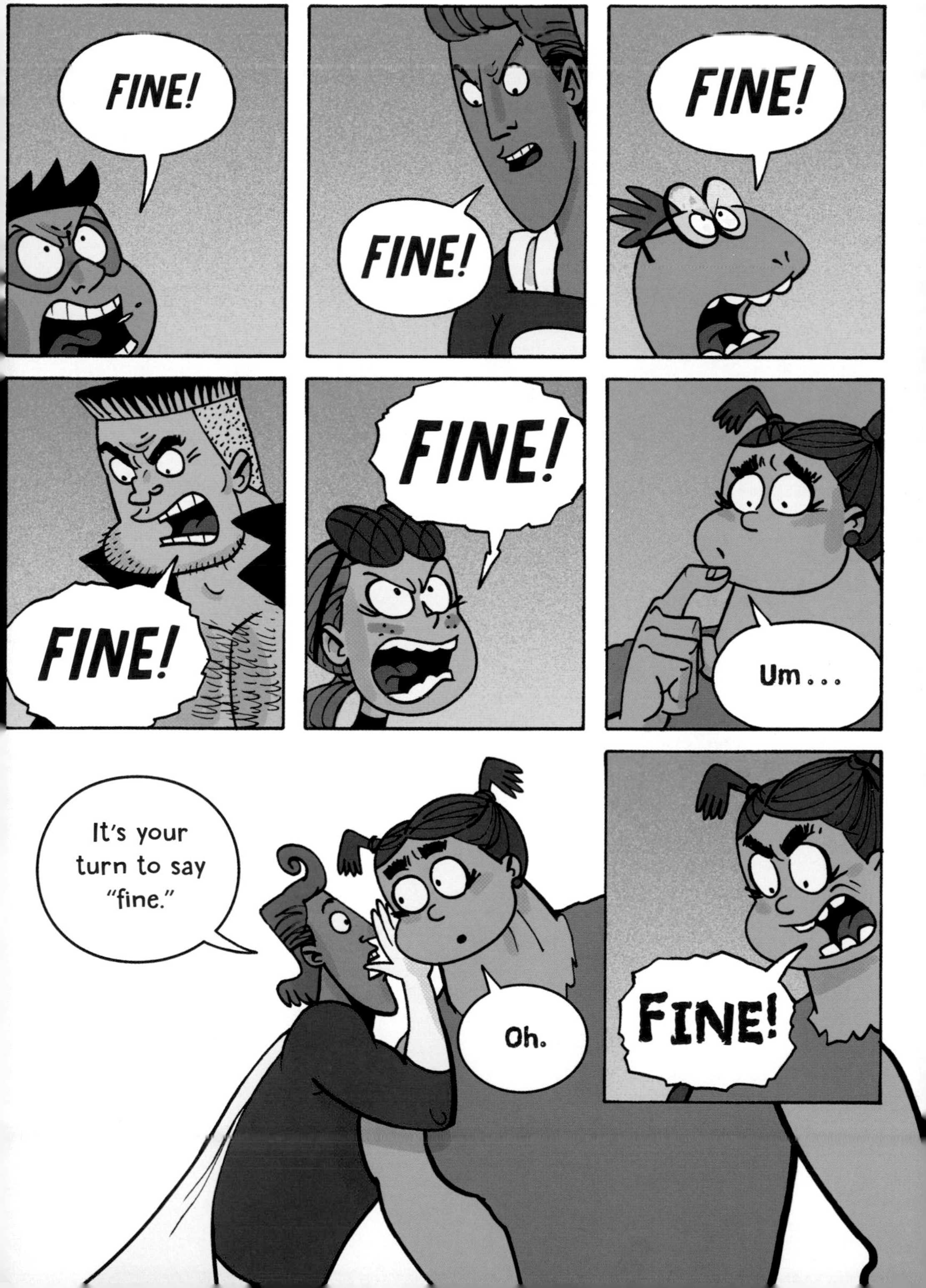
FINE!
FINE!
FINE!
FINE!
FINE!
Um . . .
It's your turn to say "fine."
Oh.
FINE!

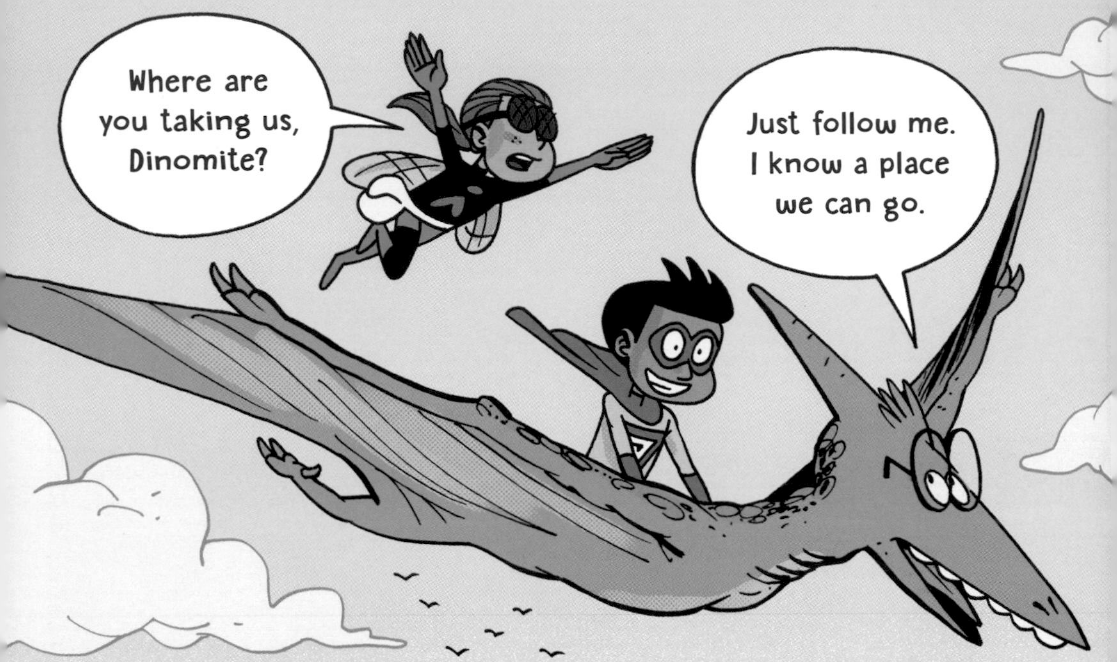
Where are you taking us, Dinomite?
Just follow me. I know a place we can go.

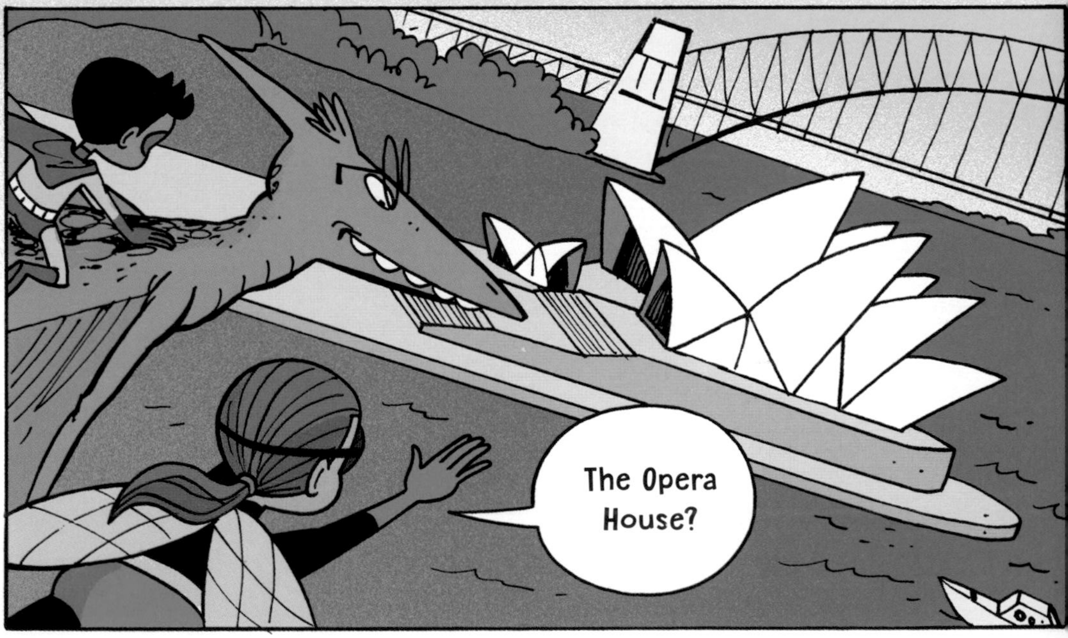
The Opera House?

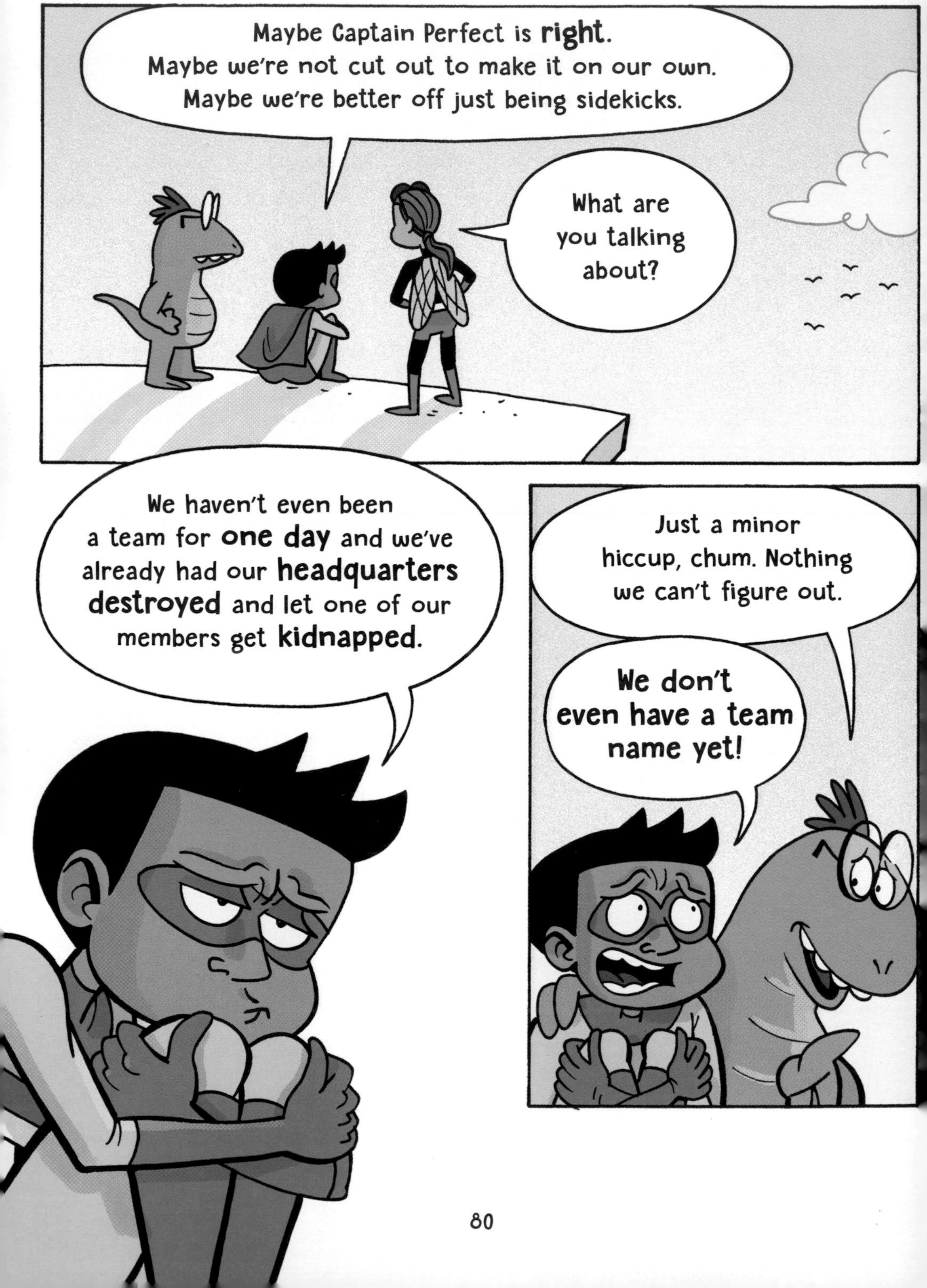
Maybe Captain Perfect is right.
Maybe we're not cut out to make it on our own.
Maybe we're better off just being sidekicks.
What are you talking about?
We haven't even been a team for one day and we've already had our headquarters destroyed and let one of our members get kidnapped.
Just a minor hiccup, chum. Nothing we can't figure out.
We don't even have a team name yet!

Dr. Enok is the **world's greatest criminal,** with an army of robot drones at his command.

I don't know if we can beat him.

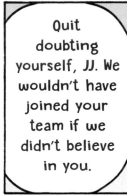
Quit doubting yourself, JJ. We wouldn't have joined your team if we didn't believe in you.

But we don't even know where Enok is.

The location of his laboratory is a complete mystery.

Junior Justice, allow me to interrupt.

I went to the trouble of placing a tracker on Dr. Enok in the middle of our altercation.

Chapter

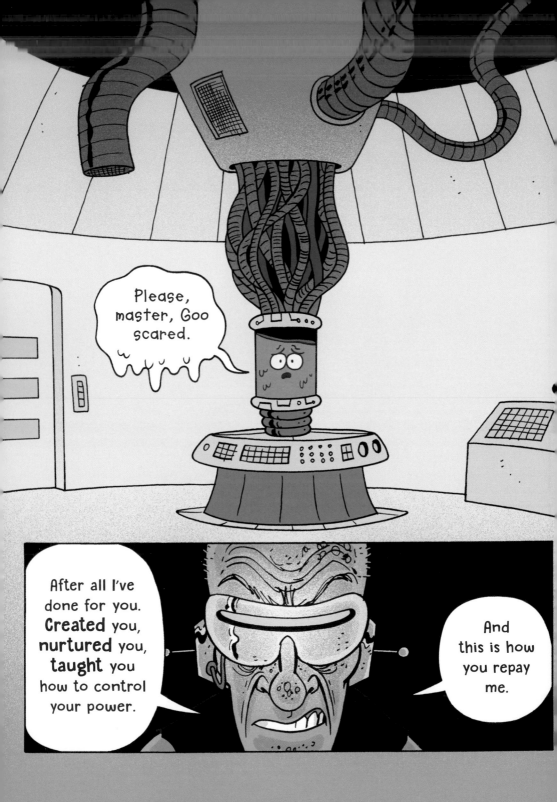

86

Hmm, you call that an apology?

TREMOR: HIGHER

WRRRRRRRRR

I've always been curious about how much discombobulation you can withstand before your molecules break down.

You seem to be reaching your limit.

Gck gck tch.

TREMOR: HIGHEST

But you know what? I designed you to be durable.

TREMOR: EXTREME!

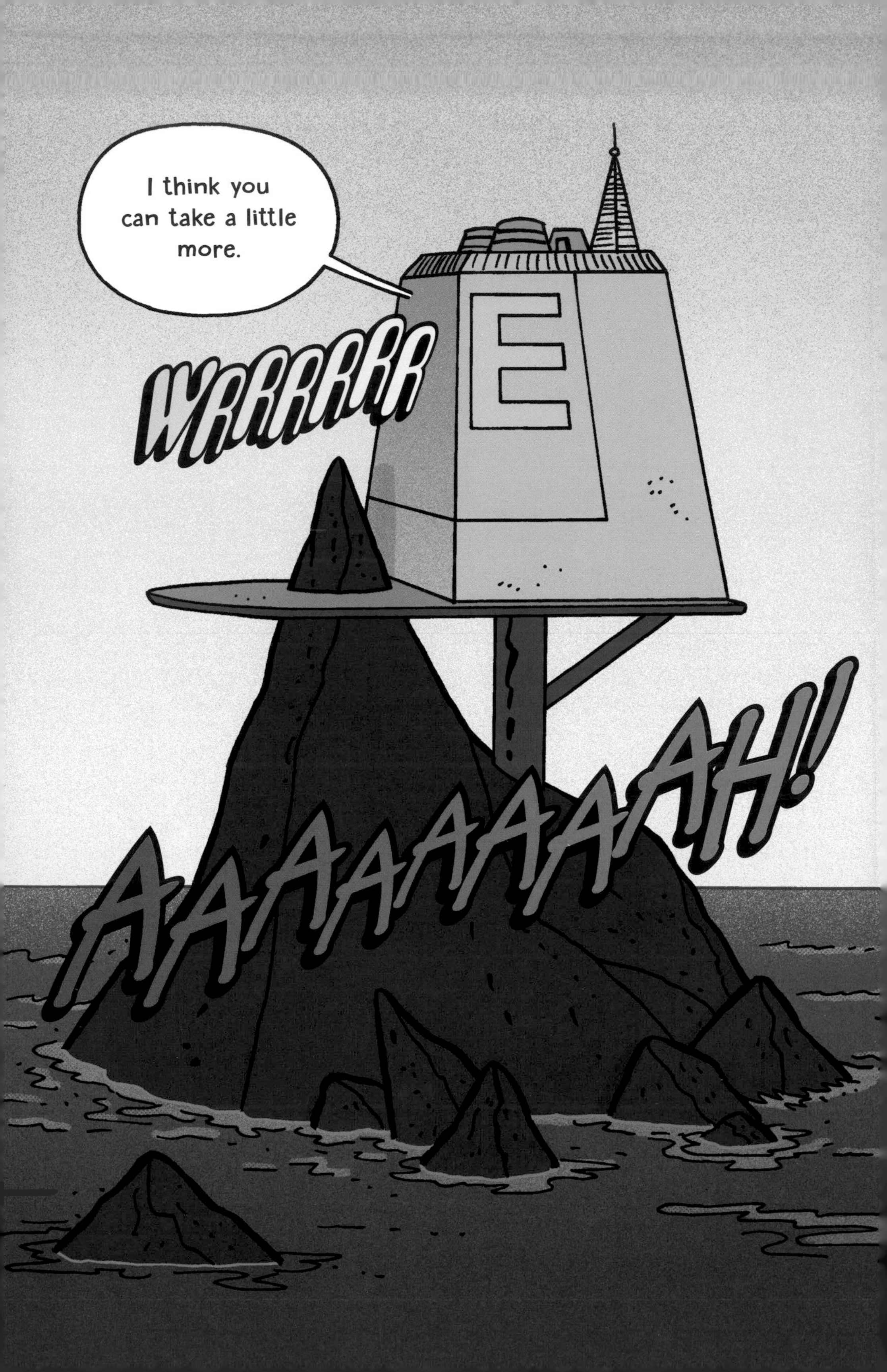
I think you can take a little more.
WRRRRRRR
AAAAAAAAAH!

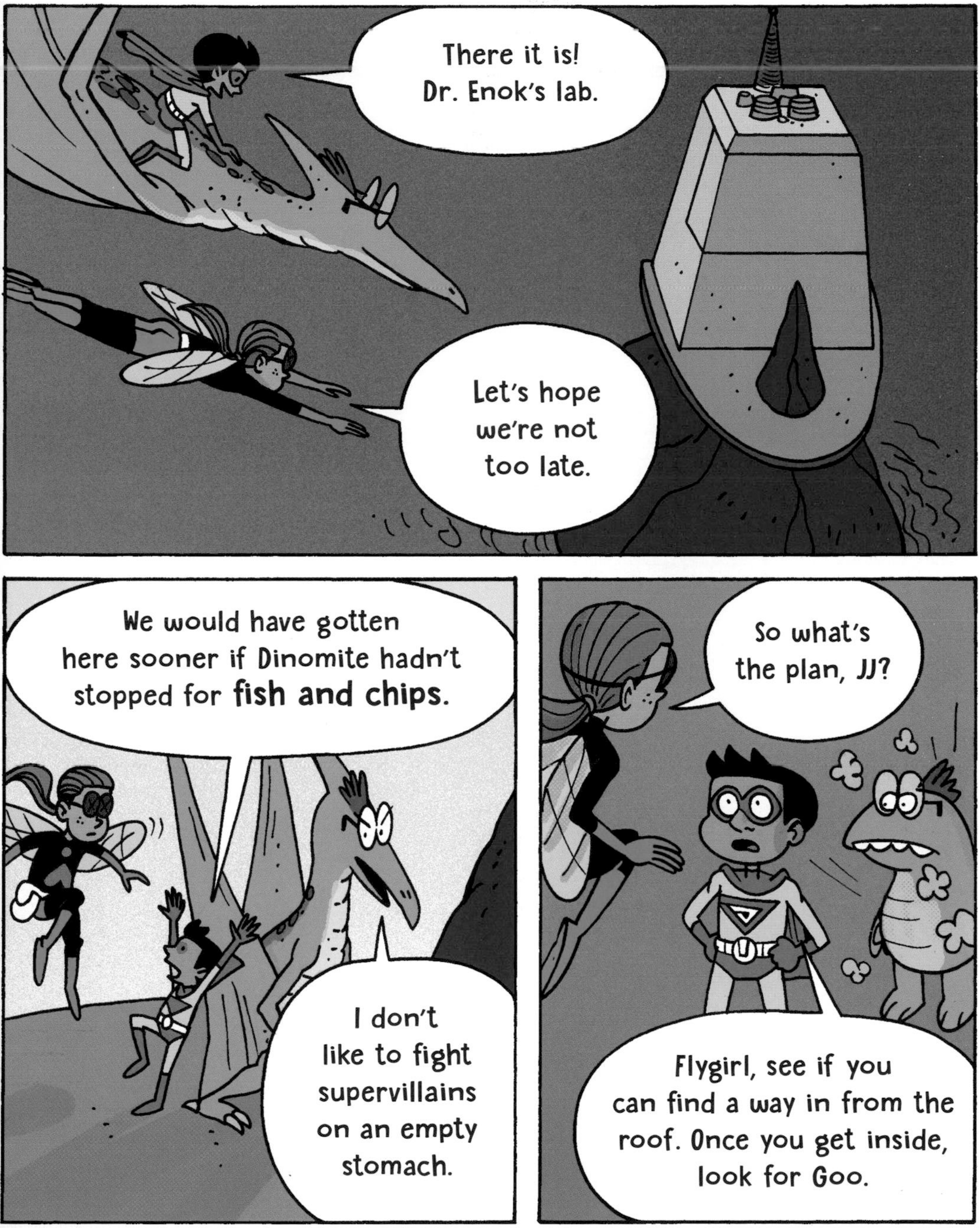
There it is! Dr. Enok's lab.
Let's hope we're not too late.
We would have gotten here sooner if Dinomite hadn't stopped for **fish and chips**.
I don't like to fight supervillains on an empty stomach.
So what's the plan, JJ?
Flygirl, see if you can find a way in from the roof. Once you get inside, look for Goo.

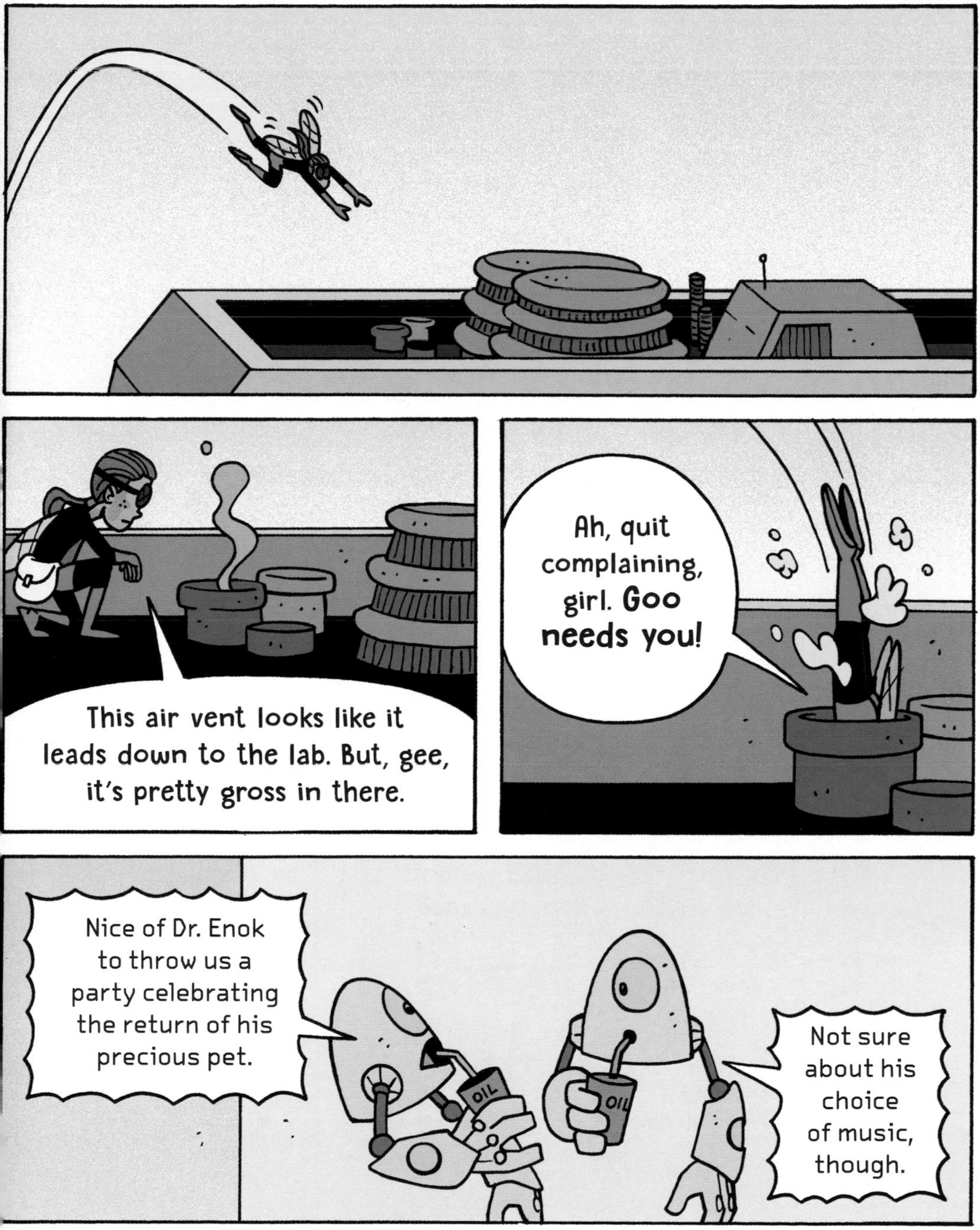
This air vent looks like it leads down to the lab. But, gee, it's pretty gross in there.
Ah, quit complaining, girl. Goo needs you!
Nice of Dr. Enok to throw us a party celebrating the return of his precious pet.
Not sure about his choice of music, though.
OIL
OIL

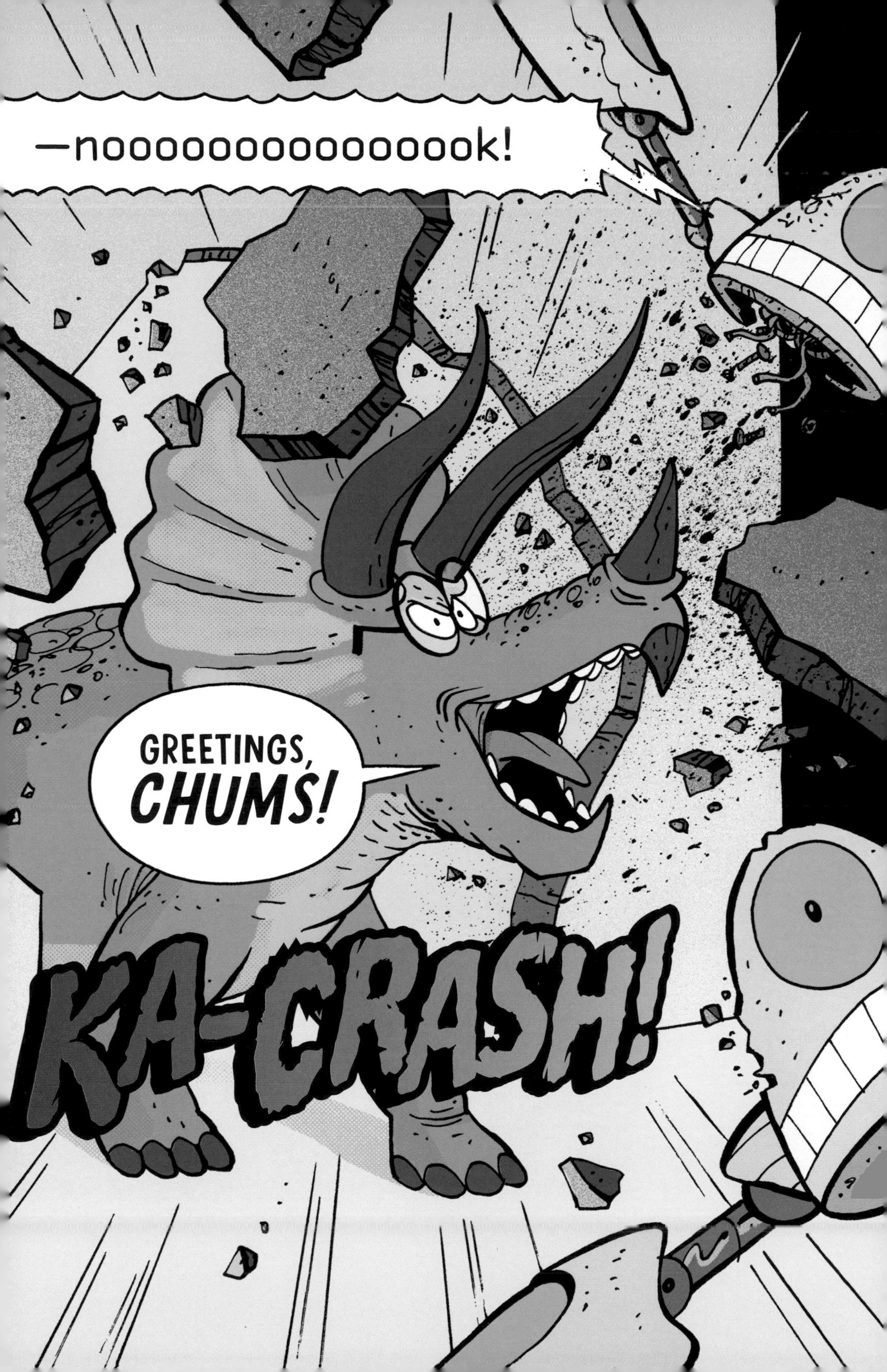
—nooooooooooooook!
GREETINGS, CHUMS!
KA-CRASH!

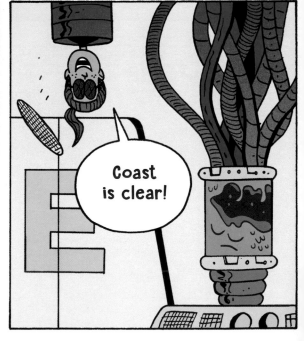

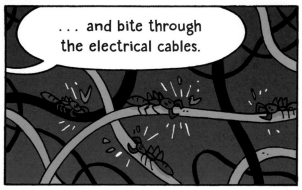

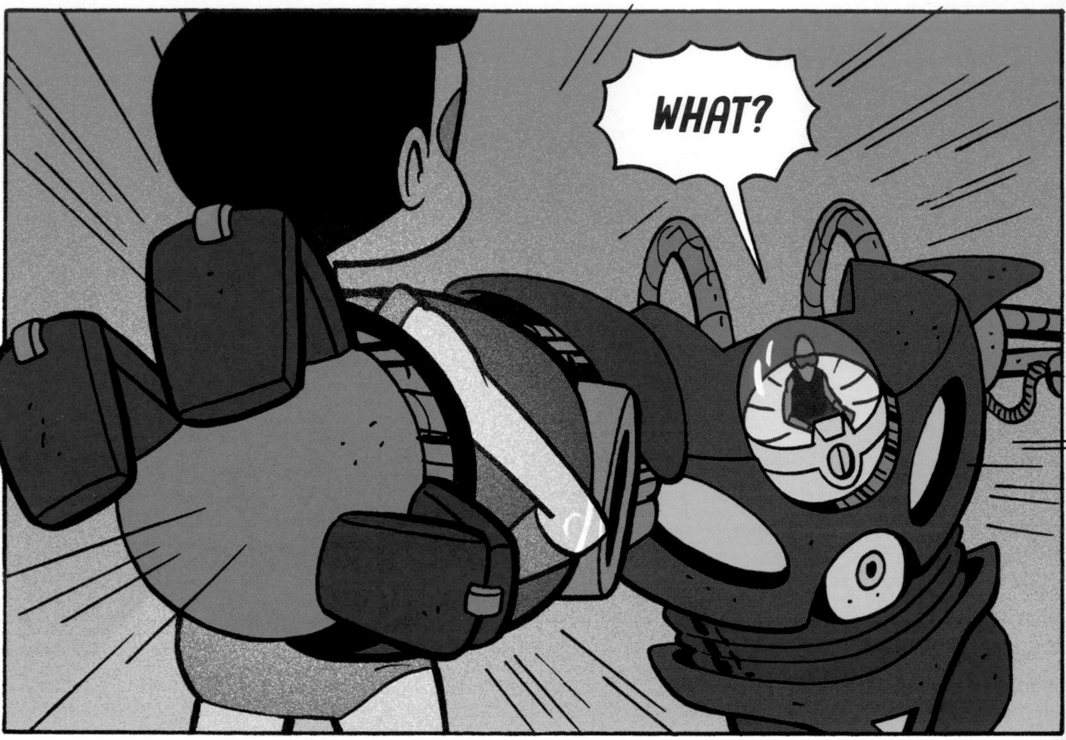
WHAT?
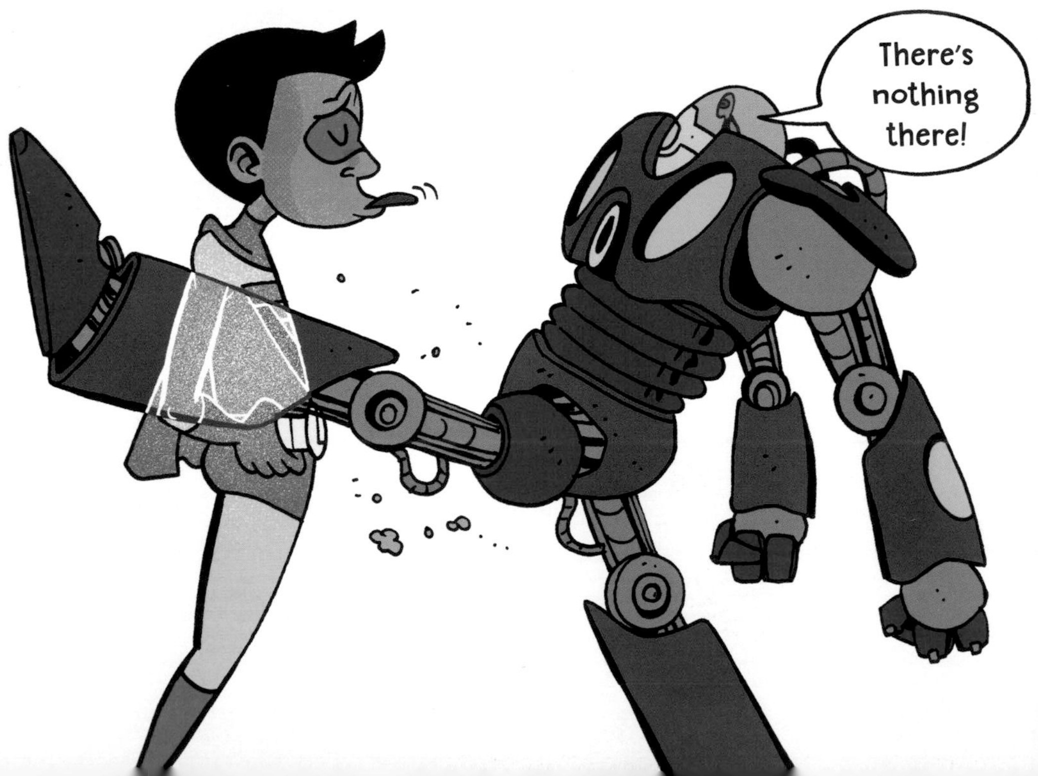
There's nothing there!

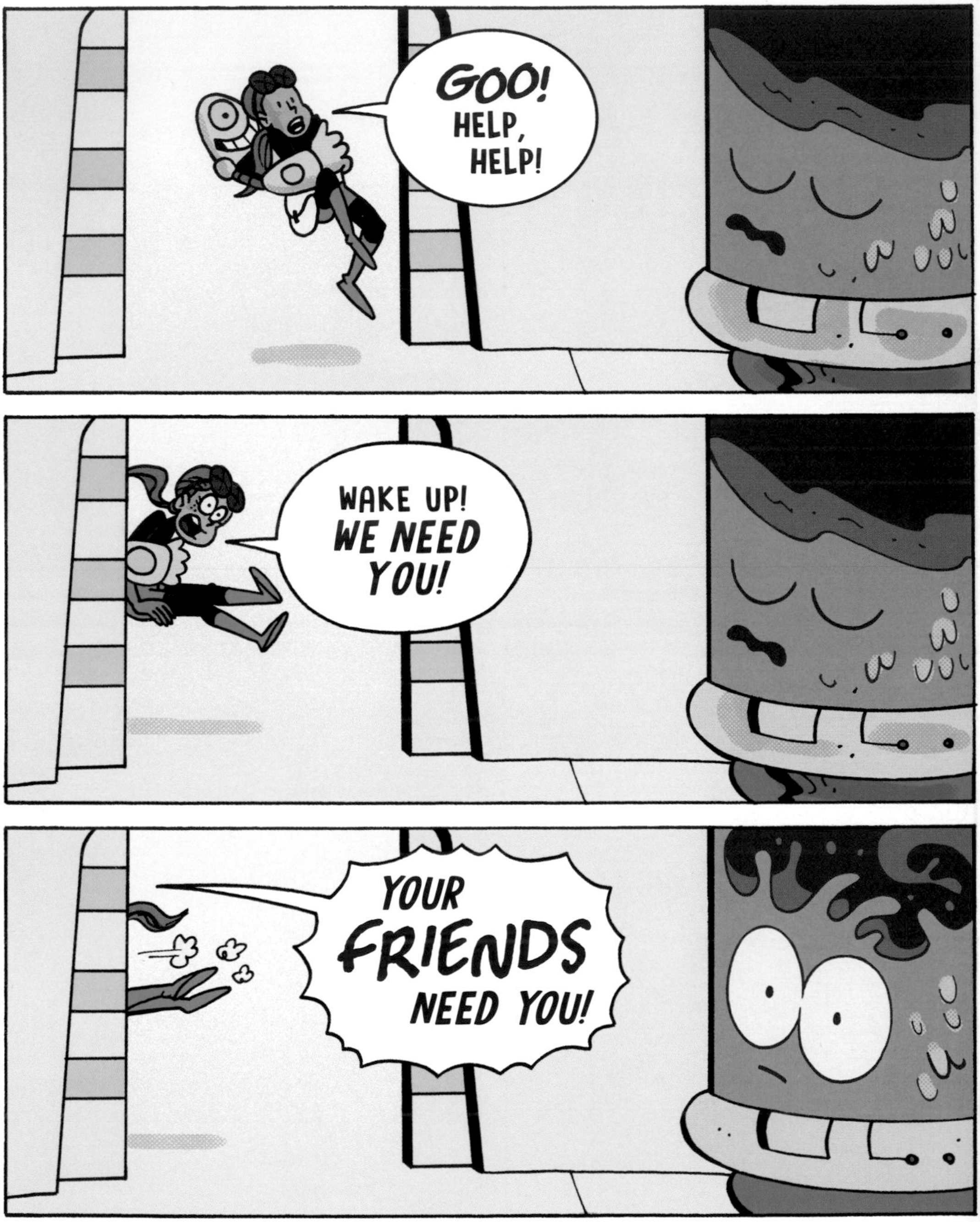
GOO! HELP, HELP!
WAKE UP! WE NEED YOU!
YOUR FRIENDS NEED YOU!

108

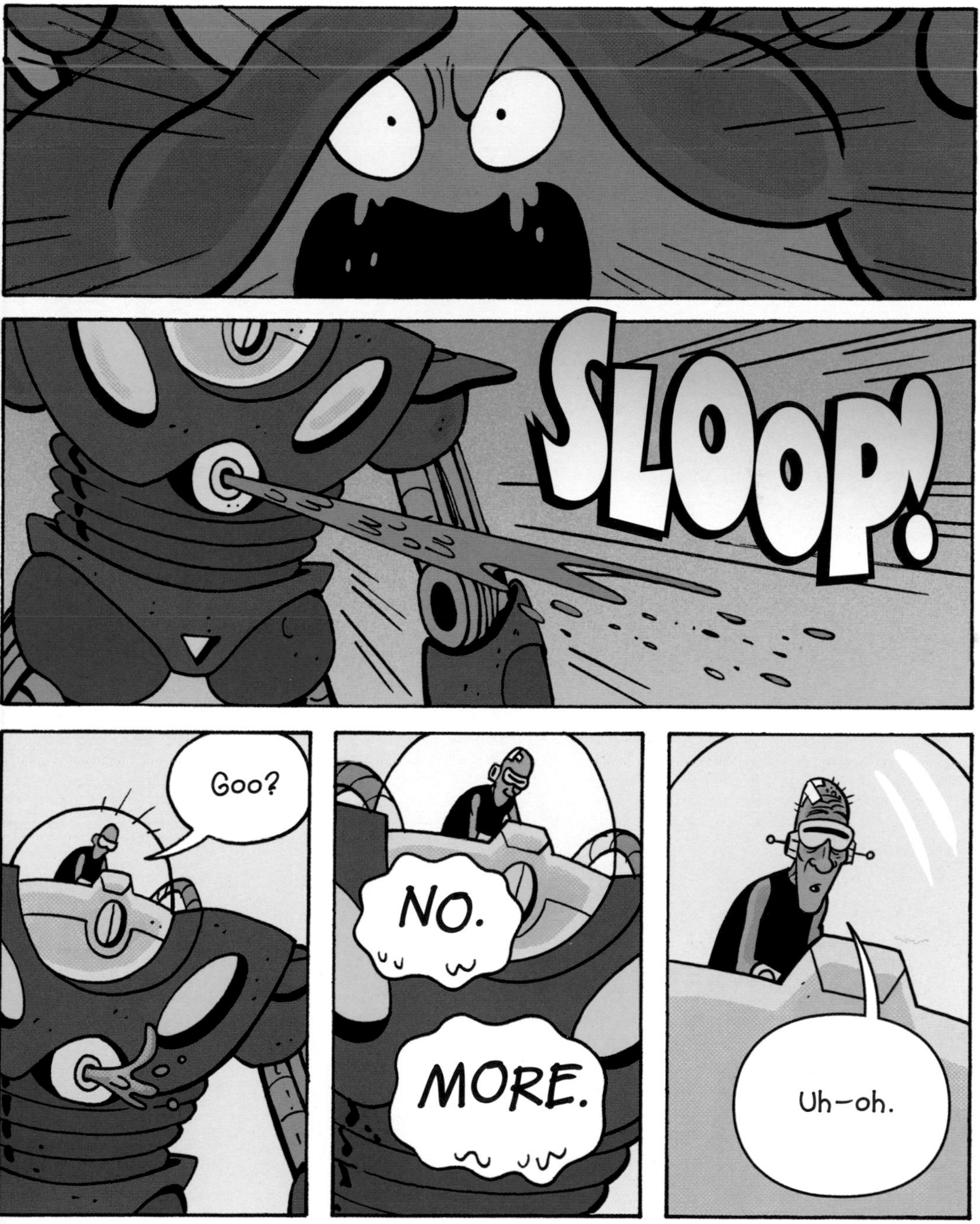
SLOOP!
Goo?
NO.
MORE.
Uh-oh.

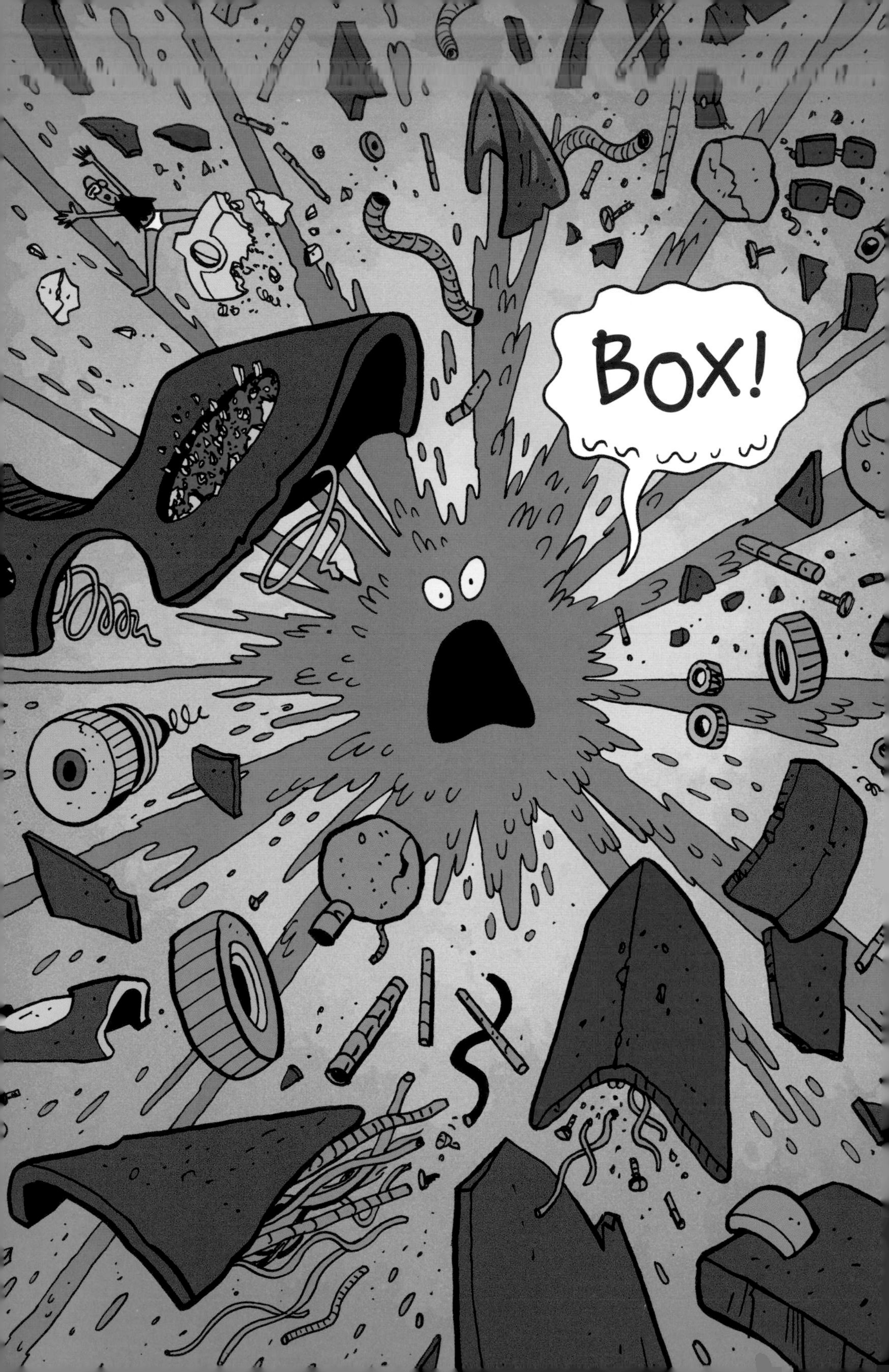
BOX!

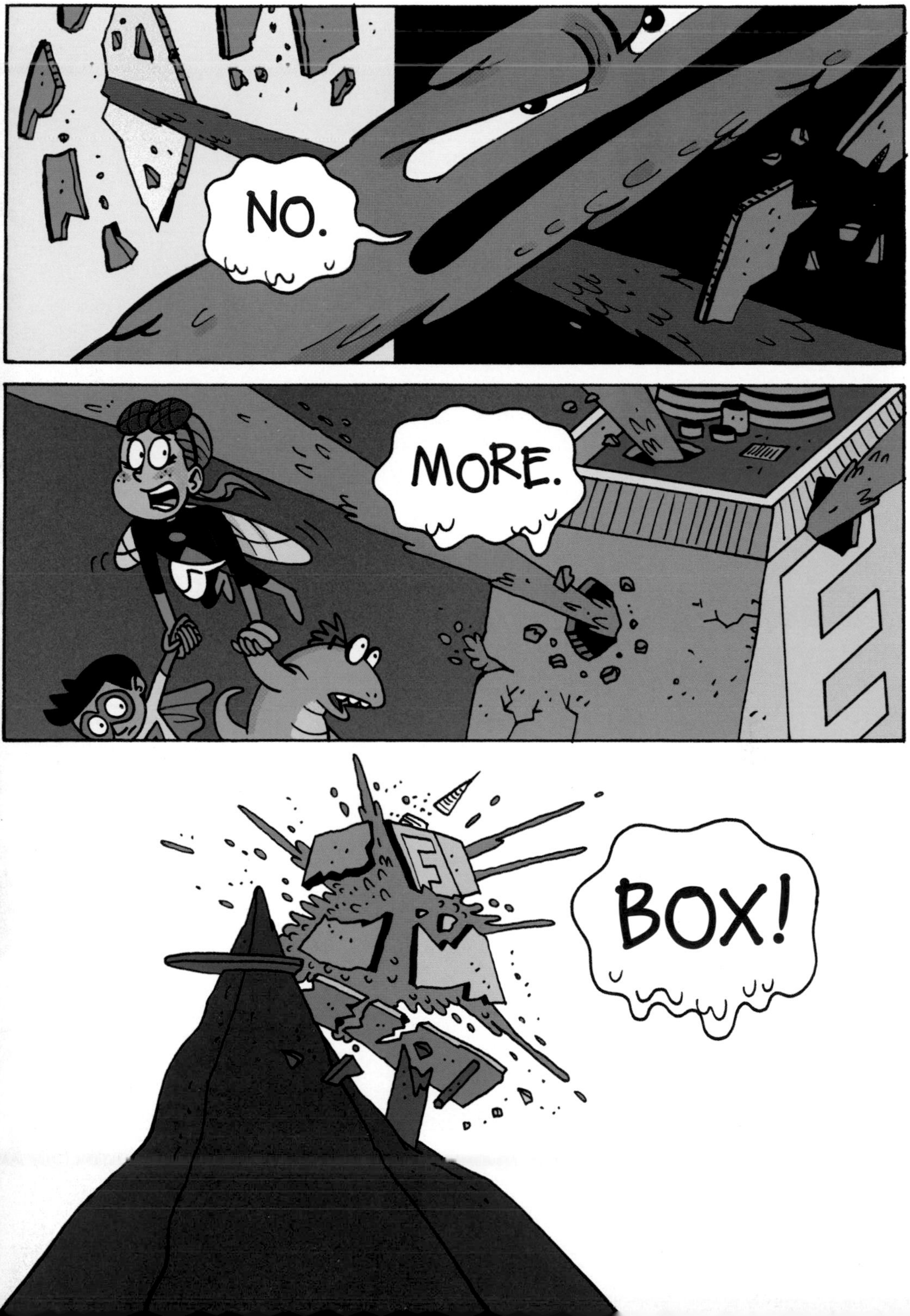
NO.
MORE.
BOX!

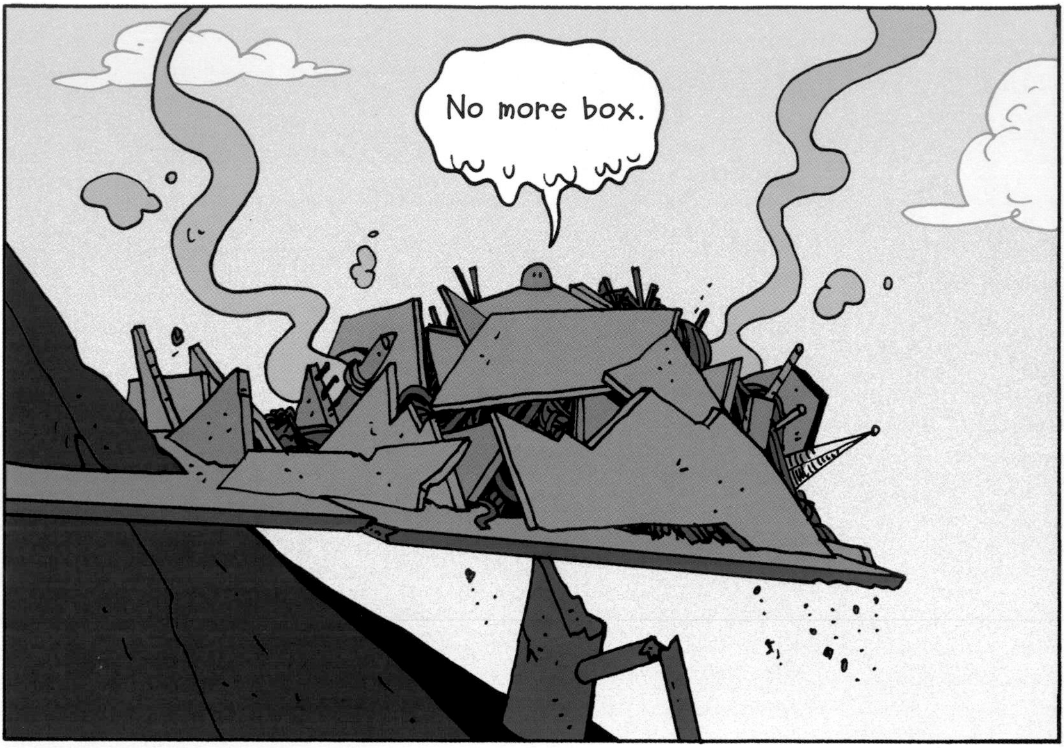
No more box.

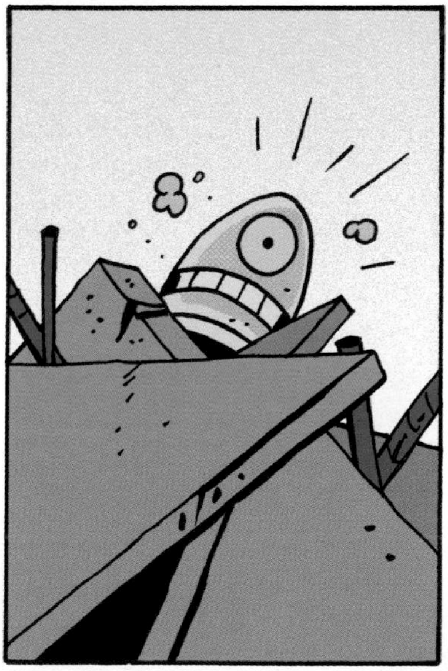

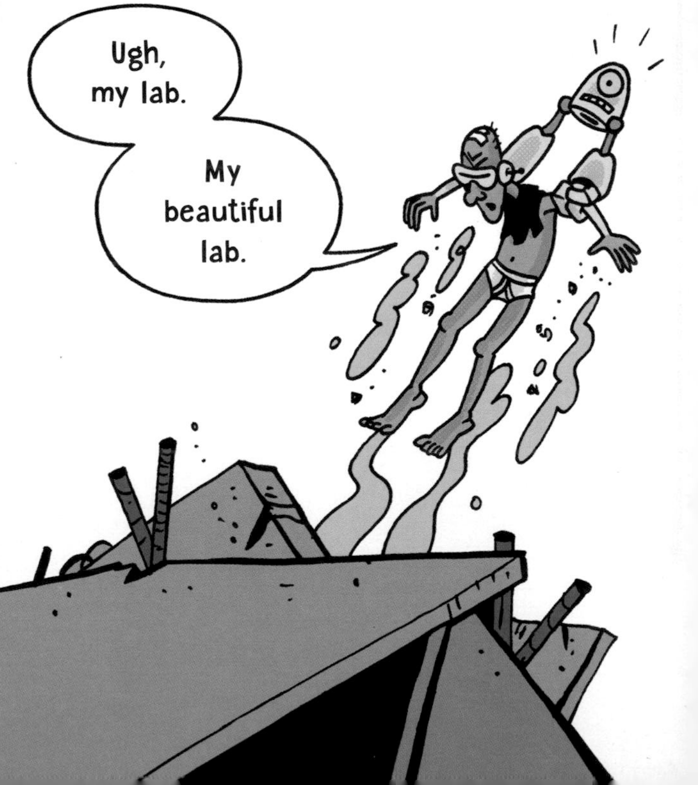
Ugh, my lab.
My beautiful lab.

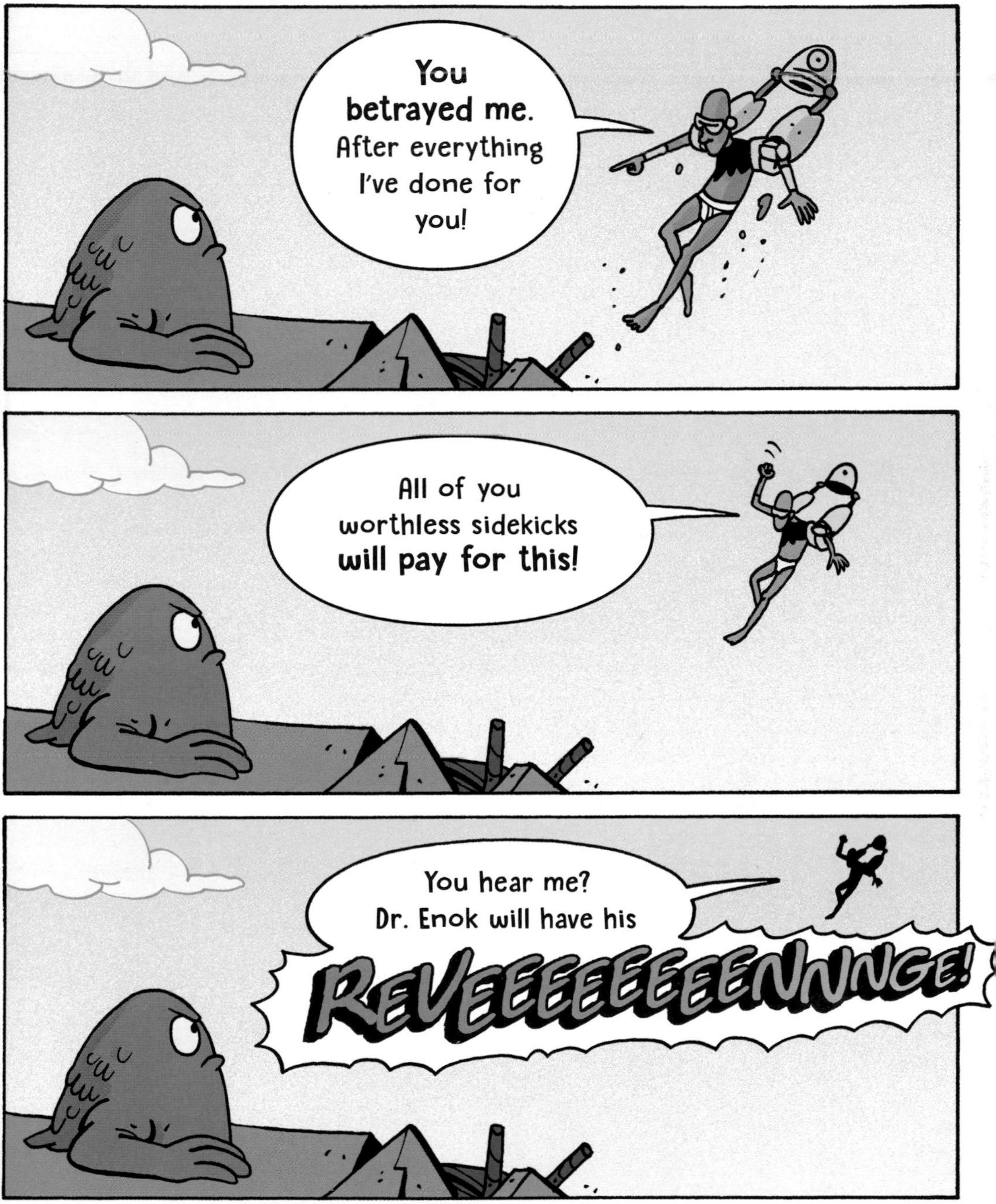
You betrayed me. After everything I've done for you!
All of you worthless sidekicks will pay for this!
You hear me? Dr. Enok will have his
REVEEEEEEEEEENNNNGE!

Chapter

124

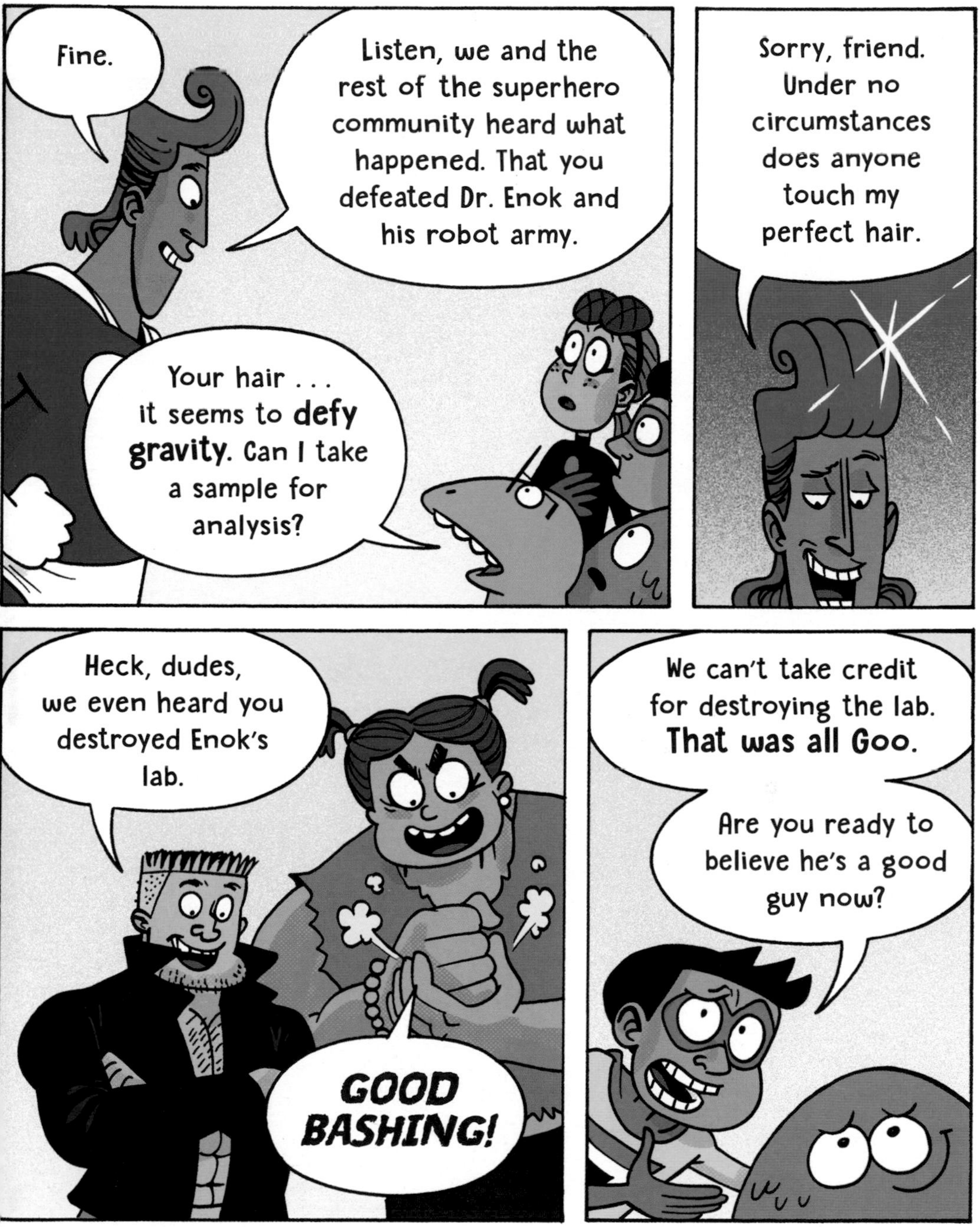

Fine.
Listen, we and the rest of the superhero community heard what happened. That you defeated Dr. Enok and his robot army.
Your hair . . . it seems to defy gravity. Can I take a sample for analysis?
Sorry, friend. Under no circumstances does anyone touch my perfect hair.
Heck, dudes, we even heard you destroyed Enok's lab.
GOOD BASHING!
We can't take credit for destroying the lab. That was all Goo.
Are you ready to believe he's a good guy now?

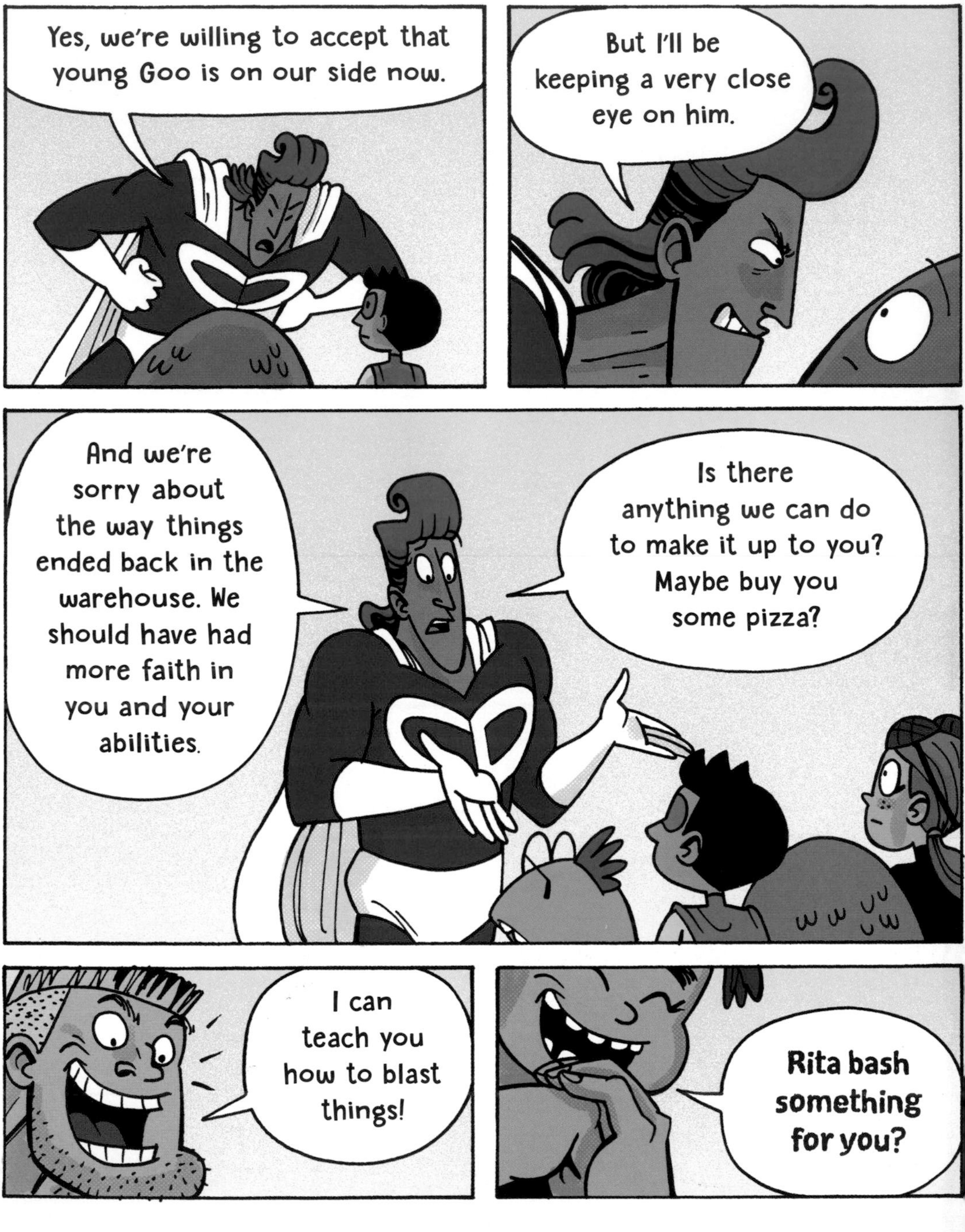
Yes, we're willing to accept that young Goo is on our side now.
But I'll be keeping a very close eye on him.
And we're sorry about the way things ended back in the warehouse. We should have had more faith in you and your abilities.
Is there anything we can do to make it up to you? Maybe buy you some pizza?
I can teach you how to blast things!
Rita bash something for you?

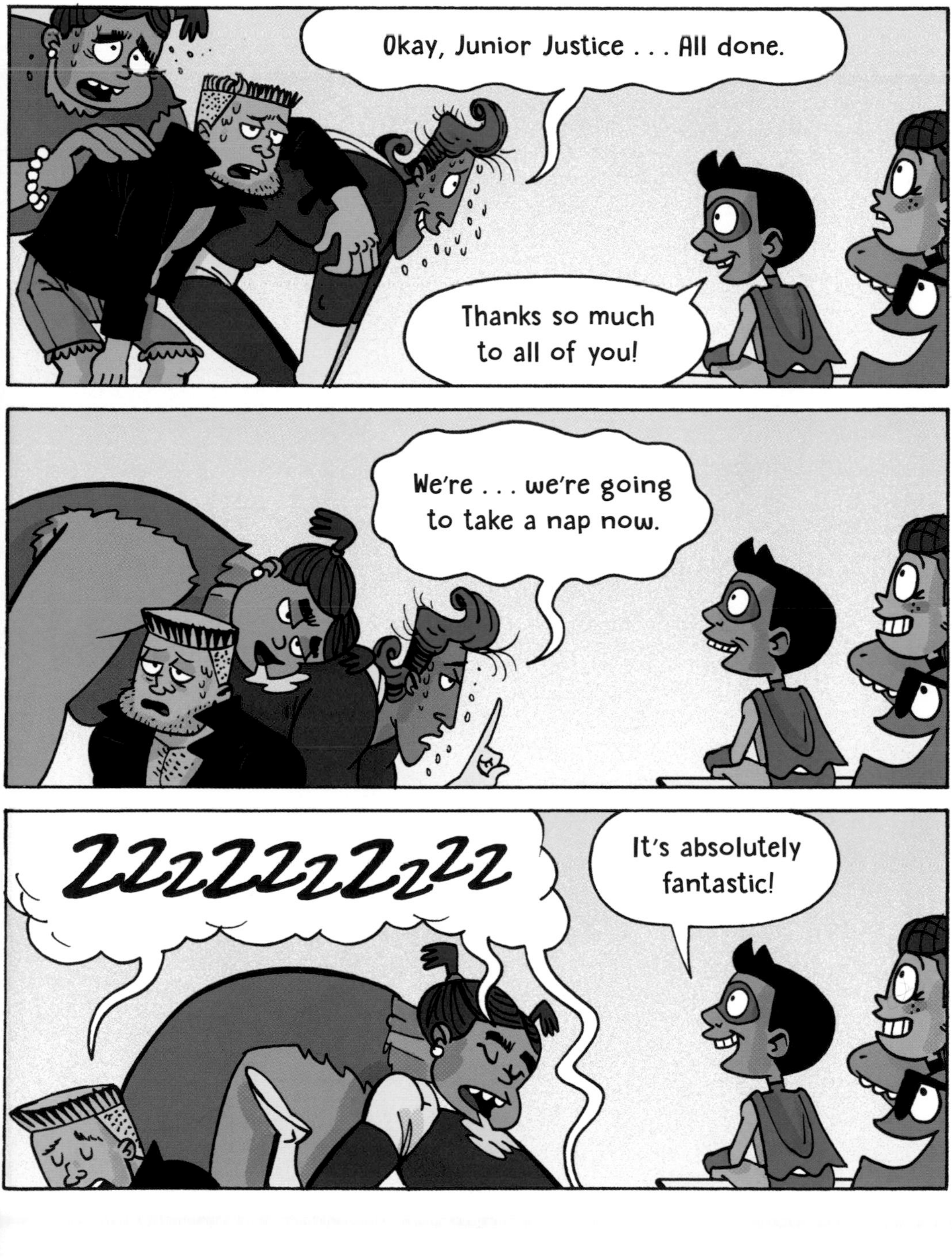
Okay, Junior Justice . . . All done.
Thanks so much to all of you!
We're . . . we're going to take a nap now.
ZZZZZZZZZZZZ
It's absolutely fantastic!

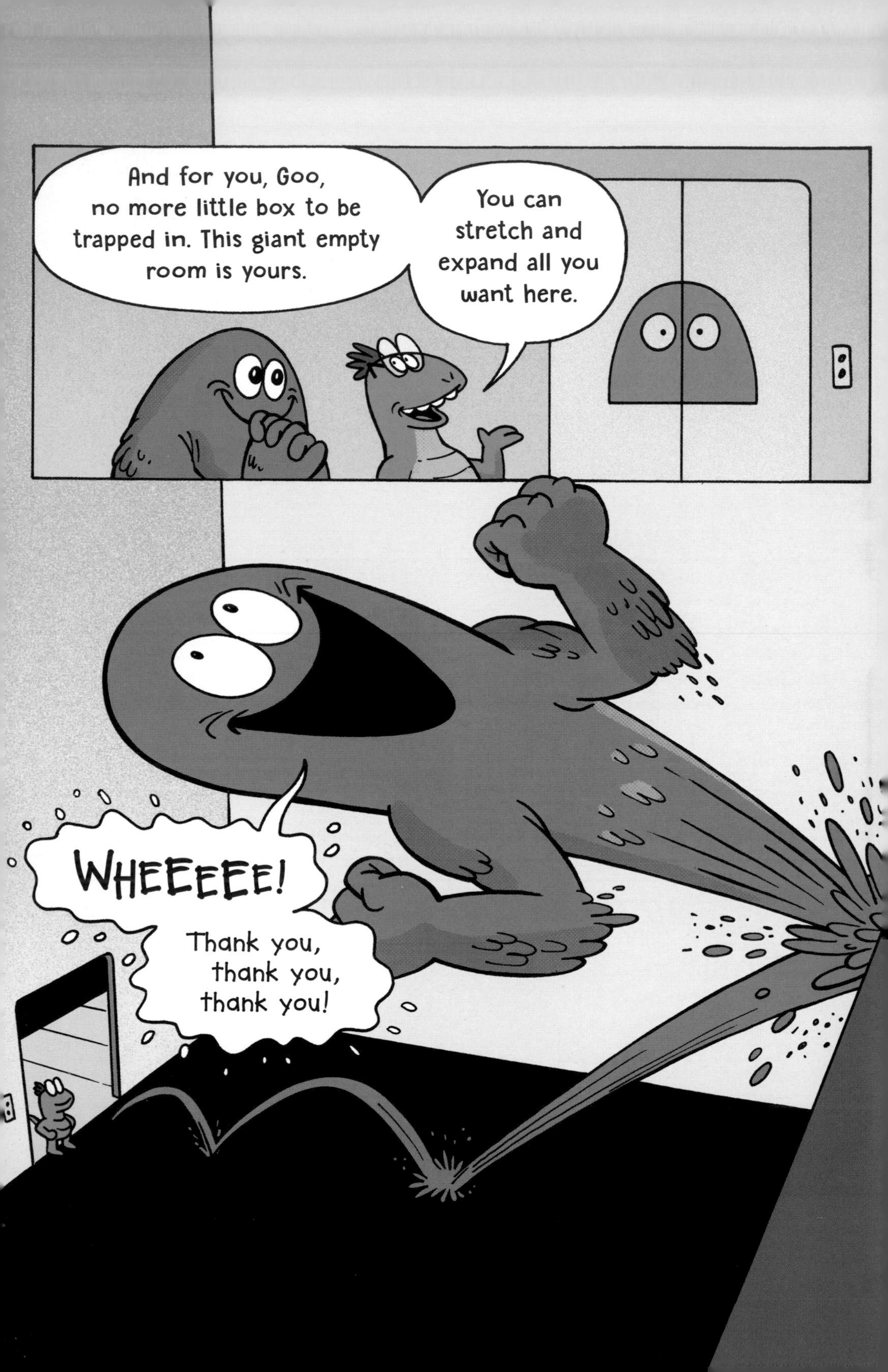
And for you, Goo, no more little box to be trapped in. This giant empty room is yours.
You can stretch and expand all you want here.
WHEEEEEE!
Thank you, thank you, thank you!

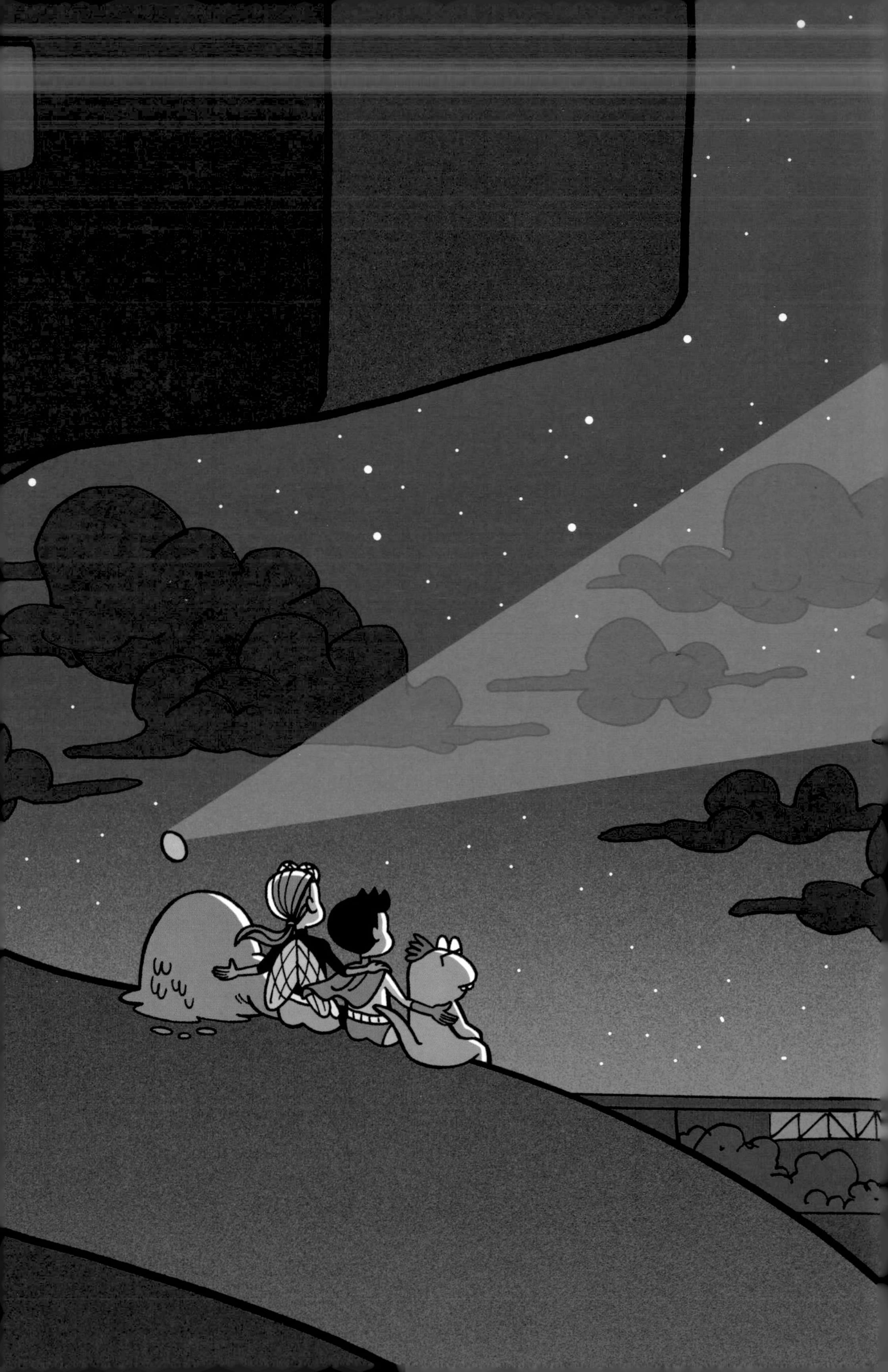

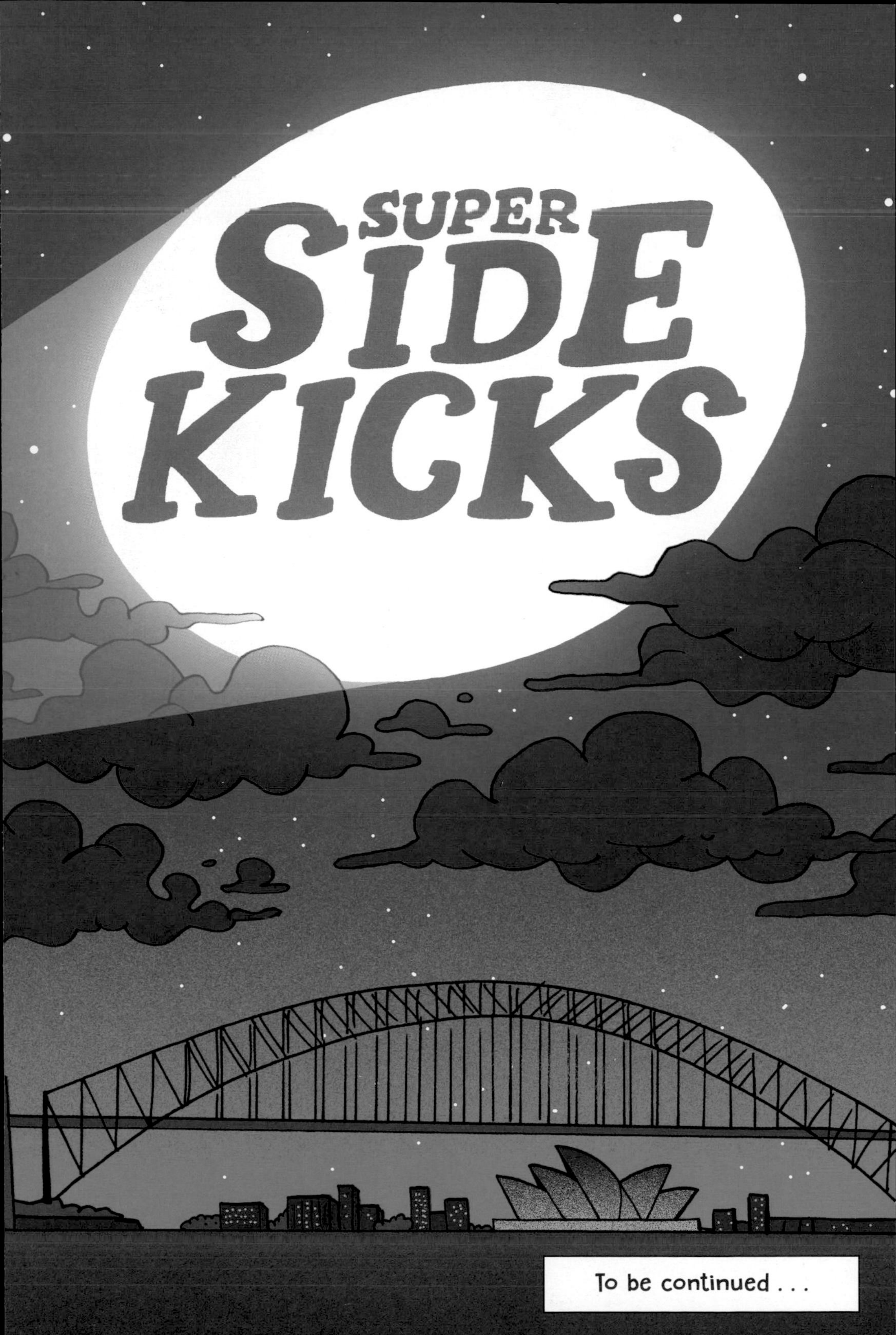
SUPER
SIDE
KICKS
To be continued . . .

GAVIN'S DRAWING TIPS

START WITH SIMPLE SHAPES FIRST: For instance, JJ is just made of circles and rectangles.

DON'T DRAW TOO DARK: Sketch lightly until you get the basic structure right.

ONE STEP AT A TIME: Once you have the structure done, it's time to draw all the cool details.

JUST HAVE FUN: Don't worry if you think you're not getting it right. Keep practicing—it takes time to get good!

DRAW JJ

1. **2.** **3.**

DRAW FLYGIRL

1. **2.** **3.**

Gavin Aung Than always dreamed of being a superhero when he was a kid. Now he's doing the next best thing: writing and drawing the adventures of the Super Sidekicks! If he could choose, he would have the fighting ability of JJ, the brains of Dinomite, the flexibility of Goo, the ability to fly like Flygirl, and above all, hair as beautiful as Captain Perfect.

You can find resources and behind-the-scenes content at Gav's website at aungthan.com and follow him on Facebook, Twitter, and Instagram at @zenpencils.

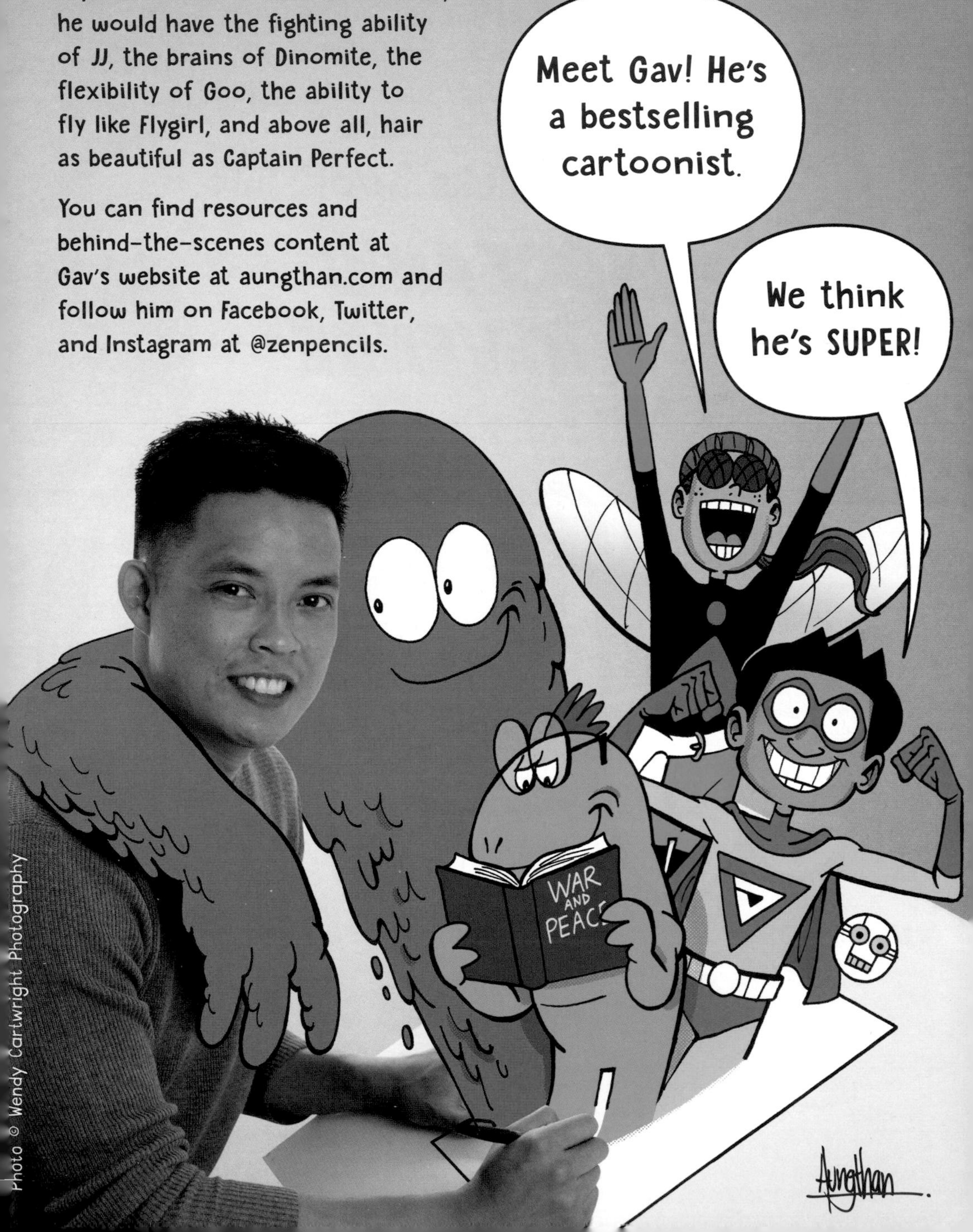
Meet Gav! He's a bestselling cartoonist.
We think he's SUPER!
WAR AND PEACE
Aungthan